# Table of Contents

a Bride for Russell
Book #5
Sons of Nora White
CYNDI RAYE

# A Bride for Russell

# by

# Cyndi Raye

# Sons Of Nora White Series

# Book #5

---

1. http://www.CyndiRaye.com

Cover art by Madison of Silverheart Publishing

# Chapter 1

Russell fumed. He stuffed his calloused hands in his pockets and rocked back on his heels. "I do not want to marry some fancy lady who doesn't know how to work on a farm!"

His mother rolled her eyes. She glanced at Nora from the neighboring ranch and the step-mother of her sons. Russell knew they had been hatching a scheme to marry him and his brother Wesley since the two women called a truce several years ago. The brothers had originally laughed it off since they had no intention of marrying anyone. Except, now it was three years later and the two women were directing their scheming towards him.

"It's time you fill the cabin you live in with a woman's touch. She's perfect for you."

Russell shook his head. "Ma, I'm old enough to make my own decisions. So is Wesley. We can find our own brides."

Except everyone knew it was a rare occurrence when the Young brothers left the farm. At their rate, it would takes years for them to find a wife!

"So be it!" Widow Young blinked rapidly as if she were going to unload a bucket of tears. Russell figured it was fake tears but he didn't have the heart to watch his mother cry. Not after all she had been through in her life and he was not going to be the reason for her tears.

"Ma, don't you dare cry! I am not adverse to marrying, I told you this before. I just don't want some big city rich girl who doesn't want to get her hands dirty. How's she going to survive here? There's no way I can make her happy! What can I give her? Jewels?" He swiped his arm in a wide motion. "Do you see any jewels here?"

The room got uncomfortably quiet after his outburst. Russell braced himself at the look Nora gave him. She turned her head and he swore, if she could, she'd turn her head in a complete circle just to startle him! That woman downright frightened him!

It wasn't that Nora was scary looking. No, she was quite a beautiful older woman. But she didn't take any nonsense and spoke her mind. Russell knew she was about to embark on a lecture with few words that meant he best pay attention. She was notorious for getting her words across.

He was right.

"Russell Young, look what you have done to your Momma! It is a sad shame to upset this woman who raised you and now all she wants is to see her boy married. How can you refuse?"

Her eyes were like daggers. Russell didn't know how to answer her. He was a grown adult yet felt about three right now. He had to make these ladies understand how he felt and yet did it really matter? They were both on a mission to see him and his brother married.

Yet, all he wanted was to see his mother smile. She had such a tough life raising them all alone with no one else. Truly, he didn't want to disappoint her. Russell turned to his mother. "I am sorry, Ma. Forgive me for making you upset." He glanced at her face, knowing he'd see her dramatic flair of turning off the tears the moment he agreed to this wedding. She knew exactly how to get under his skin. He sighed, stuffing his hands deeper in his pockets. He knew this was what she wanted to hear and was reduced to tears to get her own way. He glanced at Nora White since she was a part of it as well. "If it's so important to you, I will marry the mail order bride you chose for me."

"Oh, honey, I'm so happy!"

Clapping her hands, she got up from the table and gave him a hug. Russell wanted to take back his words but she was so darn ecstatic he didn't have the heart. He had to know something, though. "Ma, do I get the same contract my half-brothers had?"

It was Nora who frowned first and answered his question. "Luckily for Luke, Adam and Samuel, they found good women. I can't imagine the outcome if one of them had sent their bride back. Think carefully before agreeing," she told Widow Young.

Widow Young scrutinized her son. Russell began to feel uncomfortable. She had always taught him to be upright and when he promised something to never go back on his word. She was giving him that look, the one that said *don't you dare try to get out of this!*

Russell groaned. He probably would never get a chance to use any such clause in any contract if he let it up to these two.

But then she nodded, causing him to relax.

"Yes, Russell, if you would like we will put a clause in the contract that will say if either one of you decide the marriage isn't working after thirty days, then either one of you can apply for an annulment as long as there are no marital relations within that period of time. Russell, how in the world will anyone know?"

"You taught me to be honest. I'm not going to lie to you or anyone else. I feel better being able to have the same opportunity as my half-brothers." He gave them a pointed look. "You do want it to be fair, don't you Ma? Nora?"

Then he grinned.

The two older women looked at each other. "I think we've created a monster," Widow Young told Nora.

Nora gave a delighted laugh. "I believe you are right. He is much smarter than we gave him credit for."

"Thanks a lot, you two," he teased. " I need to get out to the barn, there's work to do."

"Go on now, son. We'll arrange everything for you and Miss Naomi Van-Walker."

Russell cringed at the name as he made his way out to the barn. Milking the cows was the best part of his day. It gave him time to think.

Alone.

What had he gotten himself into? Russell glanced over at the plain looking two-room cabin he had built last year across the yard from the main home. He was at the age where he no longer wanted to live under his Ma's roof. Copying the same idea that his half-brothers had done, he built a cabin near the property line of their farm with no plans at the time to get married.

Now Nora White put the idea into his Ma's head it was time they marry! Just because she was so successful in marrying off her own three sons didn't mean she had to interfere in their lives.

He growled after kicking a bucket sitting by the barn door. It tumbled and rolled towards the field.

He made his way to the small pail beside the stall. Grabbing it, he plunked it upside down beside his milk cow, Dolly, and sat down. The four year old Jersey cow produced plenty of rich, creamy milk for their family. It was his job to milk her every morning and evening. He had gotten a late start this morning because of the marriage conversation, which now he had in his head.

Russell ran a hand over the light whiskers on his chin before gently taking hold of a teat in each hand, pulling and squeezing in a steady motion. Dolly stood still except for an occasional whip of her tail. A few times she hit Russell dead in the face.

He enjoyed the quiet time in the barn before he got a start on the day. The sounds of the outside world was muffled except for an occasional rooster crowing. The cluck, cluck of hens as they cackled didn't ever phase Russell. Usually Wesley and he traded tasks so they didn't get tired of one certain job but he didn't want to give this one up. Milking Dolly was much better than trampling around the chicken pen any day!

Naomi Van-Walker! Even the name sounded uppity. Russell's head flew back when Dolly swatted him with her tail. "Now, Dolly, sweetheart, settle yourself." When he spoke to her in soft, low tones, she settled right down. Dolly was a good, quiet cow but when the flies were bad like they were this morning, her tail was flying all over the place, regardless who was in its way.

"Almost done," he told her. He grinned to himself as he wondered if Miss Van-Walker would talk to Dolly. Russell planned to teach her how to milk a cow, gather eggs and all the things they had to do on a farm. As a matter of fact, Russell was going to teach her every single chore, even the ones he never expected his own Ma to do. Then, hopefully, she'd high-tail it out of the farm life so fast he'd be left alone for good. He didn't want to disappoint his family but he didn't want to get married. Not right now. Probably not ever. He was content just the way things were.

Yet, if he chased this one off, he knew Ma and Nora would most likely find him another bride to replace her. Probably one worse. The two women were determined to see him and Wesley married.

"You got your heart on your sleeve, brother," a voice spoke out, jerking Russell back to reality. Russell pointed one of Dolly's teats at his brother, spraying milk in the air. Wesley laughed and opened his mouth, wiping his cheek with the back of his hand when it sprayed him in his face instead.

Russell loved his twin. Wesley was three minutes younger than he was so Russell always considered himself more mature and the decision maker. Wesley didn't seem to mind. He was more fun loving and even encouraged their ma to find him a bride.

Maybe Wesley would want the Van-Walker bride. Russell didn't mind waiting until last. "You want to get married first?"

Wesley laughed out loud. "I'm afraid that won't work, brother. Ma and Nora have it all planned out. Your going down the isle first."

He leaned against the post, facing Russell.

"I don't want to get married. That's the thing."

"Looks like you have no choice."

Russell frowned. "We always have a choice."

His honest statement had Wesley nodding. "Yes, it's true, but do you want to upset Ma, or even Nora, who has been good to us since she found out her husband fathered us? She did have the right to hate us, you know."

Russell turned his head, anger taking root. He hated this conversation, it made him want to cross the line to the White ranch and piss on the man's grave. That's how mad he was at his own father. He knew it wasn't Nora's fault but sometimes he took it out on her. "She didn't allow us near our own half-brothers for ten years. How do you justify that?"

Wesley leaned in. "Russell, Nora didn't know about us. The only ones who knew were Luke, Adam and Samuel. They had promised never to tell and until it came out by accident, they weren't planning on telling anyone. But Nora did right by us, why do you still resent her?"

Russell didn't want to hate. He didn't have room in his heart for hate, his mother taught him to forgive and move forward and he had. Except for this one thing. His natural father. The man took advantage of Russell's mother when she was weak. She had just lost her first husband and Mr.White came over the hill to her rescue. How was he able to go home at night to his wife and children, knowing he was with someone else?

Russell knew one thing. He knew when it was time for him to become a father, he didn't want to be anything like his own. The man taught him what kind of father not to be.

He flung a hand over his forehead, wiping sweat away. Picking up the steel milk can, he covered it to take it back to the house. His Ma would make butter this morning and he'd milk again this afternoon for some fresh milk with supper.

"Go on, Dolly, get on back outside." Wesley and Russell grinned at each other when the cow turned around in the barn and made her way outside. Russell turned to Wesley. "I don't hate Nora. Actually, I like her and am glad she called a truce to the animosity. But when I think of her husband, our father, it brings out anger and I want to lash out at her. It's unfair but the way I feel."

Wesley slapped a hand over his shoulder. "Our life was tough, but we made it through. Ma did good on her own. Don't you think it's time we bring a bride home, give her someone to talk to while we are out working? She deserves a daughter, grandchildren."

Russell snapped his jaw shut. "Wesley, is that the reason why you want to get married? To appease Ma?"

The younger brother by a few minutes shrugged. "Why not?"

Russell shook his head. "You don't marry because your Ma needs company! She can go visit anyone in town, or, Nora who is just a spit away from here. You want to get married for all the wrong reasons!"

The two made their way across the yard. "I have lots of reasons why it's good to marry, brother. Besides, Ma doesn't plan to live here forever, you know. Haven't you seen the way her and that preacher from Cooper's Ridge have been eyeing each other? It makes you wonder if she won't be married long before either one of us."

"He's too old for her."

"Nah, he's not that old. Just looks a bit rough around the edges. Heard he was a reformed outlaw before he became a preacher."

"We better keep an eye on him. He may want Ma for the wrong reasons." Russell had seen the preacher come calling but always thought it was out of kindness and church related. Shows how much he paid attention to the goings on around him.

Wesley nudged him. "Heard Miss Van-Walker will be here on Saturday."

"What! Already? I only agreed about twenty minutes ago."

Wesley laughed at the horrified look on his face. "Ma and Nora had this planned all along, didn't you realize this? I best be getting my own work done, brother, since you'll be busy with a wedding night and all come Saturday." With that, he slapped Russell on the back, chuckling.

Russell went inside to set the pail of milk on the kitchen table. His Ma and Nora were busy talking, or rather, planning Saturday's wedding reception. They began telling him right away he'd have to pick his bride up at the train station and the pastor of Wichita Falls will provide the ceremony. Then, he'd bring his bride back home to a nice reception.

Russell had way too much respect for his Ma and all she had sacrificed to raise two boys alone. Watching the happiness elude from her as she spoke with Nora made him glad he was doing this after all. Even if he wasn't crazy about getting married. He'd make the best of things and in the meantime, if it fell apart, there was always that clause.

<><>

Naomi lifted a ragged hem and shook her head. Now that she was off the train, she wanted so badly to wash the soot and dust from her and change into her fine dress.

She pushed the few coins deep in her pocket, careful not to let anyone see she had money. But when her eyes darted back and forth along the street of Wichita Falls she realized she was in a completely new place. There wasn't a homeless orphan in site. This town was not like New York City. She was no longer an orphaned urchin as the nuns at Lady Catherine's Orphanage had called everyone.

She had always had to guard any pennies that she had earned before someone bigger than her bullied her and pried them from her fist.

Naomi had learned fast. As the years went on she learned to work her way around the city, where to sleep or to hide when the truant officers came looking for children not in school. As she got older, Naomi longed for her own home, a place to put down roots. She grew tired of living in abandoned buildings and being chased out of the library after she learned how to read and write.

She pulled back her shoulders. As of this day, that life was no longer hers. Naomi Walker was now a well-to-do lady from the upper side of town who was going to marry one Russell Young, who owned his own farm.

The minute she had turned eighteen she knew what she had to do to survive. After learning to read, she swiped a newspaper and found the section where men were wanting brides to come out west to live on farms and ranches and to places where they were able to make a home of their own. She knew no one would accept a homeless orphan so she lied about her upbringing.

Naomi hurried to the boarding house where she was to spend the night. She knocked on the door to find a beautiful older lady swing the door wide open. "Come in, come in."

After a quick perusal, Miss Addie, as she was called, took her to her room up the stairs and at the end of the hall. "We have supper at seven sharp. If you miss it, I'm afraid you are on your own. Doors close at nine on the nose. If you want to sit outside on the porch after nine, you'll have to wedge the door, otherwise you are stuck out there for the night. Although, if I may, it isn't proper for a single lady to be outside alone after dark. Have a good evening."

After the woman left, Naomi swung herself in a circle. She raised her hands up over her head. This was bliss! A warm room with a bed. She flung herself on the bed, stretching out even before she removed her coat. A laugh she didn't realize she owned came out. It surprised her that she was able to.

The warm feather bed felt so good she snuggled up on her side, not even taking time to undress. Not that she had a nightdress along anyway, she never owned one. In her donated carpetbag was a single outfit for tomorrow. She had taken care it was folded neatly and placed in her bag when she left the train station in the big city.

Naomi drifted off to sleep, missing supper, thinking about her new life ahead. It had to work, there was no turning back now that she had a taste of a real bed. Her heavy eyelids closed as she smiled and snuggled deeper into the mattress.

Soon, she would meet her new handsome, charming husband.

**Chapter 2**

Naomi jumped up, realizing the sun was streaming right in her face from the lone window across the room. Her belly grumbled as she worked her way out of her ugly weathered cotton dress. On the dresser was a pitcher filled with water. Naomi took advantage, using a cloth on the dresser to scrub away yesterday's dirt.

She lifted a small bar of soap to her nose, sniffing the rose scent and closing her eyes in ecstasy. Had she died and gone to heaven? Enjoying this, she worked the water and soap through her hair, rinsing it the best she was able with the small amount of water in the basin. It wasn't like submerging herself in the stream at the park where she'd go to bath as an orphan, but at least she had sweet smelling soap.

After taking a long time bathing and enjoying every single moment, Naomi opened the carpet bag and pulled out her beautiful dress. The nice woman who ran the matrimony agency in New York gave it to her, insisting if she were to present herself as a lady of means then she'd need new clothes.

Naomi was used to wearing one dress for a long, long time. Years ago, while younger, she had even consorted to wearing boys trousers and jackets, stuffing her hair underneath a hat to hide from the vultures who looked for young girls to kidnap from the streets. Those days were over, thank you Lord!

She wanted desperately to leave her ragged dress behind but knew it had to be cleaned and brought along for the times her new one needed laundered. Staring at herself in the one small mirror above the dresser, Naomi wondered if she were truly able to pull this off. Why did it matter where she came from as long as she was able to be a good wife? Maybe she should be honest with her new husband instead of starting out a marriage with lies.

Except the lady at the matchmaking office said it would be better for her if she at least acted as if she were from good breeding.

Otherwise, he may send her away without any means to come back. Naomi wondered if the matchmaker realized she was used to being rejected, to living on the streets. But she wanted this one chance to have a home where she belonged, so she went along with the lies.

Taking a deep breath and a last look in the mirror, Naomi made her way downstairs to where a few renters were already having breakfast.

"Welcome, Miss Van-Walker."

Naomi smiled. "I'm terribly sorry I'm late for breakfast. I also apologize for not being at the table yesterday for supper. I sat down on my bed and fell asleep instantly."

Miss Addie gave her a knowing look. "Most travelers almost always miss their first meal. It's a tiresome ride."

"I didn't mind the ride at all."

"Well, have a seat and help yourself."

Naomi sat down, picking up a napkin and placing it across her lap. She wanted to tuck it into the neckline of her dress but after reading the book at the library called True Politeness, A Handbook of Etiquette for Ladies, she knew her napkin was to be placed on her lap. It was oddly stupid she thought. How was she going to protect her beautiful dress from stains on her bodice? Her mouth was up top not on her lap!

After staring at a platter of beautiful, round flapjacks that made her want to drool, she heard Miss Addie's voice in the background but didn't know what she had said.

Naomi hated turning away from the delicious looking fare. "I'm sorry, would you repeat that?" She forced herself to look away and pay attention.

Miss Addie tilted her head. "You may help yourself. Charles, can you please pass the pancakes to Miss Van-Walker?"

The man across from her picked up the plate and held it out. Instead of taking the platter, Naomi reached across with her hand and picked up two flapjacks, placing them on her plate.

When she looked at the man to say thank you, his eyes went wide and his mouth hung open. He cleared his throat. "Uh, very well, then." Setting the plate down, he excused himself and left the table as if in a hurry.

Too late, Naomi realized what she had done. Miss Addie had an amused look on her face but didn't mention the fact she had just made a big mistake. So used to grabbing for food, even in some of the soup kitchens in New York, Naomi was so hungry she had reacted like an urchin. Like the homeless poor girl she was.

Filled with dread, she tried to act as if she hadn't just used her hands to pick up food. Instead, she picked up the pitcher of syrup and commenced to dribble it over flapjacks she ,desperately longed to devour.

Using the fork and knife, Naomi tried to be delicate and picked up a small piece, inserting it in her mouth. The delectable flapjack melted in her mouth, its buttermilk taste causing her to moan out loud. A chuckle beside her made her look over to see a young man nodding his head. "They are delicious, aren't they?" he added, then got up and left the table.

After the first bite, Naomi didn't care about etiquette any longer. She dribbled even more syrup on the cakes and shovelled them in her mouth like a starved animal. At one point, her cheeks were full until she chewed and swallowed the whole lot.

When her own plate was empty, she glanced at the flapjacks left on the platter in the center of the table, oblivious to anyone watching her. When she finally looked around, she realized everyone had gone except for Miss Addie who sat at the head of the table with a bemused look on her face.

"I'm sorry, I ate like a vulture." She had seen how vultures ate dead carcasses many times in her homeless days and knew she was acting exactly like them.

Miss Addie set the cup down on her lacy tablecloth. "You are not from 5th Avenue, are you Miss Van-Walker?"

Dread reared its ugly head. It was obvious her ruse was up. Now what would she do, where would she go? She hadn't even made it to the Young Farm yet! Naomi was a failure. Her shoulders slumped. "Am I that terrible an actress?"

Miss Addie nodded. "I'm afraid so, dear. Although, I can read people much more clearly than most. Your new husband may take you at your word, but I've been to 5th Avenue and know better." She studied Naomi for quite some time. "Now, we don't have much time. Finish up. You may have the last of the flapjacks before we head out to the mercantile."

"Wait, what do you mean?"

Miss Addie checked the time. "Your future husband will be here at four this afternoon to take you to your new life. I suggest you come along with me because we have some work to do. Your dress is beautiful but you will need a hat, which I am assuming you do not own?"

"No, ma'am." Was there hope she may pull this off?

"Just as I thought."

"Why would you help me deceive someone?" Who was this woman who saw right through her?

The older woman steepled her fingers together on the table. "Miss Van-Walker, I've been around for a long time. If there is one thing to learn here in Wichita Falls and the surrounding area, the people here love second chances. This town is built for those who want to leave their past behind and start over. I don't know your story but I am certain you want a new life or you would never have agreed to become a mail order bride. This is the place to make it happen. We take care of each other here. You will see."

Naomi never in her life had someone say these things to her. She had thought she'd be alone even in her quest to start over and make a new life for herself.

To be someone of importance.

Even to find love. "I don't know what to say. Thank you." The biggest issue going through Naomi's mind was trusting someone other than herself.

Miss Addie seemed to read her mind. It was perplexing. "Your secret is safe with me. Unless you purposely hurt someone, I will leave it up to you to be honest and you will know the right time to come clean."

Naomi nodded. "I will come clean, I promise."

Miss Addie stood, nodding to a young lady who entered through the back door. "We will be gone for a few hours, Angelica. Would you mind clearing the dishes?"

Angelica waved them off. "You go on, Miss Addie. There is no reason for you to ever have to do dishes, that's why I am here."

"It's a lovely thought, Angelica, but I've been working since the day I opened this place. I won't have it any other way."

Angelica turned and smiled. "Not unless you marry that handsome fellow you've been courting."

Miss Addie picked up her hat from the rack, placing it on her head. "Come along, dear. I'm not indulging this young woman any longer."

Naomi longed for the type of relationship the two ladies had, bantering back and forth like sisters. She hugged herself, realizing she was in a good place. If it weren't for the good Lord above keeping an eye on her, Naomi wouldn't be here to witness their bantering. She'd make sure to be grateful for whatever came next.

The next two hours were spent at the mercantile as they went shopping. Going through a rack of ready made dresses, Naomi thought those were the only kind there was until Miss Addie explained most people stitched their own or had them made to fit.

"In due time, you can learn how to sew your own clothes."

"I know how to tie a knot and stitch but I've never sewed my own clothes," Naomi told her. "I'd be willing to learn. I want to be a good wife who can sew, cook and take care of a family." The only gift she had was surviving on the street. She wasn't sure that was helpful here.

"I'll teach you to sew. Every Tuesday afternoon, if you can, I'll put away some time for you. If you don't show up next Tuesday, I'll know you have no interest in learning."

"I promise to be here. I want to learn."

"Good. Gather your dresses and add this wide-brimmed hat to your pile. This is my treat. You will need something to keep the sun out of your eyes."

Naomi picked out a gingham day dress, along with a striped taffeta day dress with Miss Addie's approval. The hat would be perfect for her wedding day, it matched the dress she had on.

As they made their way back to the boarding house to wait on the buggy that was to come pick her up, Naomi began to get nervous. Was she able to pull this off? She glanced at Miss Addie, an older woman who seemed to know every single person in town. Why was this woman of means helping her? Did she have a motive? Naomi wasn't used to anyone offering her a helping hand without wanting something in return.

Life on the streets made a person not trust, period. Even those who had promised to help had a motive. One time in the city, a grocer had caught her going through a trash can out back and threatened jail. Then, he changed his mind and told her to come back on Saturday and he'd give her free food that was left over from the week. She had gone each Saturday for a few weeks until one time he tried to put his hands all over her.

Luckily, she had street smarts and got away, taking a heel to his knee. She learned her lesson that day, never to trust anyone, especially those who were being nice. They always wanted something.

Yet, she didn't have the same feeling with Miss Addie. In a way, it was easy to let her guard down with the older woman. Of course, she'd never been in a town so far removed from the big city before either.

She wanted to trust the woman, but still, she had to be careful and not let her guard down. Even though the woman walking beside her had offered to help, Naomi was certain that sooner or later, she'd want something.

At the boarding house, Miss Addie turned to her. "We'll have tea and a sewing class next Tuesday. Will Tuesday suit you?"

Naomi worried her bottom lip. "I don't know. You sure are helpful for someone who doesn't know anything about me." There, she said what was on her mind. May as well get it off her chest right now.

Miss Addie laughed. It was a genuine, hearty laugh. She turned to Naomi. "I have faith you will always do the right thing and that includes telling your husband-to-be the truth about your past. If you wish to practice on me, I'm all ears."

"There's not much to say, really. Since you've already figured me out, I'll be honest. My home has been the streets of New York City. A few months ago I was picked up by truant officers and placed in St. Catherine's Orphanage but when I turned eighteen they sent me right back into the streets. That's when I decided I wanted something more."

Miss Addie nodded. "I figured as much. Don't be hard on yourself. Let's get your clothes put away. I have something for you for your travels to the Young Farm."

She followed the older woman to her room, where Miss Addie pulled down a rather handsome carpetbag from the shelf. "This is for you, leave the other one in the room and I will discard it. No one will ever believe your story if you carry that worn out bag."

Her gift brought tears to Naomi's eyes. She was hardly able to conceal them. "I'm not sure why you are being so kind to me, but, thank you."

Miss Addie nodded, embracing the young lady. "You will learn, Miss Van-Walker, that I care about everyone who comes through my doors. Now, get your things together, your groom-to-be will be here in less than an hour."

She was right. Naomi glanced at the clock on the wall. Time was ticking away. She hurried up to her room, taking one long glance at it and began to fold her beautiful dresses. Pulling out her copy of the Ladies Etiquette book, she shoved it between two dresses in the new bag. This book was pure gold and she needed it for guidance since she had no clue how a real lady should behave. Perhaps in due time she'd tell her husband where she really came from. Today, her top priority was getting through the next few hours.

"I believe an angel fell from heaven."

No one answered him. It was because he was alone, in the buggy, sitting in front of Miss Addie's boarding house staring at his bride-to-be. When she walked through the front door and stood on the porch, his mouth fell open in surprise. Russell closed it but he blinked twice. How'd he get so lucky?

Clearly, he had misjudged his two mothers and their ability to find him a mail order bride he wouldn't dislike. The woman standing there was waiting for him.

Him.

A simple farm boy who wasn't real interested in a wife.

Until now.

With strands of thick blonde hair flowing from under a wide-brimmed hat, he wanted to tear it off her head and run his fingers through her hair. She wore a beautiful dress that brought out the color of her eyes, and he noticed her smile seemed genuine. He was expecting a snooty, uppity city girl.

It was when she looked up and he was able to look into her eyes that he fell, hard. She drew him in like no other had ever done. Without another thought, he got out of the buggy and made his way to the front porch, desperate to get closer to this beautiful woman.

Taking off his hat, he turned away for a split second to nod to Miss Addie who stood by her side. "Ma'am."

His eyes went right back to those blue orbs. What did it matter if she were some spoiled rich girl? He wanted her. For his wife. Today. The pull was so strong it startled Russell. Had he been out on the farm too long?

No.

There were a few women from church that were always sweet on him but he never wanted any of them like he wanted Miss Van-Walker. Without her even saying a word, he knew she was the one.

How did this happen?

"Mr. Young?" The older woman's voice sounded amused.

He had been blatantly staring into Miss Van-Walker's deep blue depths. She stared right back, her eyes bold. Her smile genuine.

He straightened, crushing the brim of his hat between two fingers. "Forgive me, I'm simply astounded by your beauty."

She simply smiled at him.

"Hello," she said, her voice almost a whisper.

A red blush began to work its way to her pale cheeks. Maybe he was being too forward. He held out a hand in an attempt to smooth things over. "I'm Russell Young. It's a pleasure to meet you."

"Mr. Young. A pleasure for me as well." She attempted to remove her hand from his when he realized he had her hand encased in his own.

Reluctantly, he let it go. Holding out his arm, he grinned. "Well, we may as well get to the church. Let me escort you there."

His bride-to-be took a step back, gazing at Miss Addie. Was she afraid? Of him?

Miss Addie quickly moved to her side. "It's your moment," she told her, giving her a hug. "I'll come along and witness the nuptials."

When the older woman offered support, it prompted Miss Van-Walker to take his arm. The three of them strolled along the street of Wichita Falls, entering the church as if they were going to a Sunday morning meeting. Several people were crossing the street, making their way to work or to the local café while Russell was about to be wed. No one noticed it was a big day for him and his bride to be.

Not that he cared. He was about to marry the most beautiful woman on earth. She had a smile that made him weak in the knees and her eyes, they looked into his soul as if she knew every aspect of him.

How in the world did he get so lucky?

Maybe this mail-order-bride stuff wasn't as bad as he originally thought.

# Chapter 3

It was time to be the sophisticated city girl she claimed to be from the letter she made up at the matchmaker agency in New York City. Naomi had tried to mimic some of the actions of the well-dressed ladies she remembered from the front of the theatre. Many nights she watched them, observing from a hiding spot in the alley across the street.

Now, she moved her hands the same way they had and it seemed to be working until she lifted her chin a bit too far in the air like she had seen the fancy ladies do, causing her wide-brimmed hat to flap back and forth in the gentle wind.

"Whoa there," Russell murmured. If he hadn't grabbed the rim, the poor hat would be tumbling down the street.

"Oh!" She righted the hat as best as she could, then behaved as if it hadn't ever happened. Trying to recall instructions on how to react from the Ladies Etiquette book, she hoped to have behaved correctly.

Miss Addie daintily coughed beside her, indicating she was not. When Naomi glanced over, the older woman mouthed the words thank you and nodded towards her husband-to-be.

With a deep sigh, she realized the instructions she recalled were for something else completely. The rules and regulations were so mixed up in her head right now. She was certain it had to do with her nerves.

When Miss Addie nudged her again, she turned to him. "Thank you for catching my hat."

He patted her arm with his free hand, its warmth surprising Naomi. His touch made her feel safe. Oddly, she didn't fear what was ahead, not even if he found out she had lied to him about who she really was. For now, she wanted him to believe every single word she had written in that letter. She needed him to believe she was a good choice for him.

He deserved a good woman. One who was from good breeding, not an urchin like herself. Naomi decided right then not to reveal what kind of life she led before now. She was too ashamed for him to find out she had been tossed aside as a child. He must never find out she was an orphan.

She looked over at Miss Addie, who glanced at her with a raised brow. Almost as if she knew what Naomi was thinking. Uggg! How can this be? Was she one of those mind readers?

While the preacher was talking, she vowed to God she would do everything in her power to become the kind of wife her husband needed. She'd learn to cook, clean, bake and do whatever farm women do. When she thought about her earlier conversation with Miss Addie, Naomi felt a bit guilty knowing she was about to go back on her word.

Miss Addie had to understand. If people came here to start over then why couldn't she? No one had to know about her past? If she was able to push it under the rug and forget that person ever existed, why tell anyone?

Naomi would have to talk with the older woman next Tuesday when she went to learn to sew.

"I do," the groom said, gazing at her.

Naomi's eyes widened. She hadn't heard a word of the ceremony. "I do, too," she blurted out, unsure now of what had been said.

A gasp came from the preachers side, where a portly woman stood holding a bouquet of flowers. She raised them up over her face to hide her expression.

Miss Addie spoke up. "It's nerves. Continue, Pastor Connors."

The ceremony was repeated, this time Naomi tried to follow along. When it was her turn she repeated the words, "I do."

They faced each other.

"I now pronounce you husband and wife. You may kiss the bride, Mr. Young."

He did. Boy did he ever! When his soft mouth covered hers it surprised Naomi. Shocked, she placed both hands on his jacket, not sure if she should push him away or pull him closer.

It was her first kiss.

Ever.

Well, then, goodness gracious, she was going to savor this kiss! No one had wanted to kiss a ragged, unruly girl with dust and city smells all over her. But now, with her face clean and her hair shiny, along with new clothes, for once in her life she was kissable.

So she leaned in and enjoyed every single bit of his kiss.

Until the pastor cleared his throat.

Reluctantly, Naomi's new husband stepped back, still holding her hand. He gave her a smile. "Hello, Mrs. Young."

"Please, call me Naomi."

"Only if you call me Russell."

"I'm not sure what it is about this church but that was one of the longest kisses ever in this sanctuary." Pastor Connors closed the good book held in his hands.

"Oh, come now, they're youngsters. Let them enjoy one kiss." The Pastor's wife scolded him. The pastor seemed to be surprised that his wife spoke up for the couple. She was usually so quiet through the many weddings she always attended.

Miss Addie congratulated them both. "You best be on your way. I'm sure Widow Young has plans for a lovely reception as soon as you both return."

As they left the church, Naomi didn't feel any different than when she entered. Except her lips felt as if they wanted another kiss from Russell again.

They went back to the boarding house so her new husband could load her carpetbag. As he helped her onto the seat in the buggy, their hands brushed and dark eyes met bright blue ones.

"I'm so happy," he told her, his dark eyes gazing into her own. "I'll be honest. I wasn't expecting such a lovely bride."

She lifted a hand to his cheek and smiled. "Thank you. And I was not expecting such a fine husband." Her heart skipped a beat at his confession. As long as he didn't expect her to be brutally honest, she was safe from him ever learning she was not the woman he thought she was. It hadn't been hard to lie about her past on paper. That was easy. But living a lie, it was going to be a challenge.

As they waved to Miss Addie, Wichita Falls faded from the landscape as they made the hour long trek to the Young Farm.

Russell seemed content to hold her hand in his own, not saying much at all. She was glad in a way. Fascinated at the miles and miles of grass, tumble weeds and blue skies with puffy white clouds looming so close overhead, her heart was in her throat at the beauty of the Texas landscape.

"It sure is lovely here," she mentioned, turning to watch his profile. He had strong features, dark hair cut short except for a few unruly places where it fell over his brow. Whiskers ran along his lower cheek and chin and he ran his fingers across them now and again.

He took his eyes from the road to catch her staring. A dimple creased in his right cheek when he grinned. He squeezed the hand he held. "It is home. There's no other place on earth I'd rather be."

They passed a gate with a newly painted sign that read White Ranch. After a few minutes he turned onto a narrow road with no sign or name that led to a large well-kept home and a barn twice the size of the house. There was a log cabin setting to the right where the buggy headed, across the yard from the house.

"Is this your home?"

"This cabin is where I live, yes. My Ma and brother live in the house. The cows and horses live in the barn. The chickens live in that pen over there when their not running around the farm so beware of a large rooster who likes to chase pretty ladies."

"Are you trying to scare me, Russell?" She was always up to a challenge. After all, nothing much scared her after living on the streets of New York for so long. There was always a way to hide or beat the odds against you.

He patted her hand, then helped her from the buggy when they stopped. Taking her carpetbag in one hand, he guided her to the front porch and up the two steps. When he stopped she almost tripped over her feet. "Oh!"

Russell gave her a wicked look before coming straight for her. He threw the carpetbag down, picked her up and kicked open the door to the cabin. Her feet dangled as she placed her arms around his neck, holding on for dear life. He carried her across the threshold and plopped her down inside.

Her breath was taken away at his brazen act. His hands were still around her waist and she wasn't quite sure what to do now. Before she had a chance to wonder, he dipped his head and whispered against her mouth. "Welcome home, Mrs. Young, my beautiful bride."

Unable to speak, her heart and mind were filled with so much emotion. Home. She wanted to look around to see her new place but his strong arms still held her there, almost against him. He closed his eyes and that's when she knew he would kiss her again.

Sweet heaven above! Another brazen, sweet, heart-stopping kiss from this man's lips was going to be the end of her!

And long, too. She didn't know how long she stood there in his arms while he kissed her like no one had ever kissed her before. For the second time in one day!

She was in heaven.

When he managed to pull away, she stared at him, her blue eyes looking at this man in wonder. What was it about him that made her feel all giddy inside?

She barely knew him. Did love happen like this? Was she in love already? She had no clue. Without a mother or father to guide her or look up to, she didn't really know how to have a relationship with anyone. All she knew was this was a whole new life for her, a new way of living right here, in this two room cabin.

"I'm sorry and yet I'm not," Russell told her, his voice low, husky. She wondered about that as well. He was staring at her in a way no one ever had before.

Then he let her go, taking a few steps back. "I don't want to scare you," he told her, his voice surprisingly back to normal. "We should introduce you to my Ma and twin brother."

Naomi didn't say much as Russell went for her carpetbag, dropping it into the other room. She was too busy rubbing her fingers over her mouth where he had kissed her a moment ago. Had he not liked those kisses? He had stopped so quickly.

Now, he seemed to be avoiding her. "I'll be back momentarily. Make yourself at home while I unhitch the buggy."

Naomi knew that was important to take care of the animal first but a feeling of panic was rising to the surface. What if he found her kisses abhorrent? Then what? Would he send her back like it said in the mail order contract? She remembered when it was read to her at the matchmakers. They both had thirty days to decide if the marriage would work. If not, and if they hadn't consummated the marriage, either party could file an annulment.

Naomi paced back and forth while her husband was busy outside. She had to do everything in her power not to let that happen. How in the world was she going to keep her husbands attention if he ran off when they kissed?

She knew there was more to consuming a marriage than kissing. Elisa, her one orphan friend tried to explain the birds and the bees as she called it but mostly Naomi had covered her ears. She wasn't ready then for that kind of jibber-jabber.

Naomi now wished she had listened.

While Russell took care of the horse, she walked around the small cabin, admiring the furniture, the walls, even the cook stove. She twirled around in a circle, her arms open wide with her head flung back. It was all hers. An actual home of her own!

She studied the ceiling. Made of wood, it was the most beautiful wood she had ever seen. She no longer had to huddle in a small space to keep warm and dry. This roof would protect her from the elements.

She did bite her lower lip when she saw the stove sitting in the middle of the cabin. Hopefully, she'd be able to watch Russell light it because it looked tricky and complicated.

Since she didn't have a clue how to light the stove, she'd have to behave like those rich city girls who never worked a day in their lives. They always had someone to do their work for them. She'd have to pretend she never did any type of manual labor before. At least until she was able to learn how to be a good wife on her own by watching and learning.

Miss Addie promised to show her how to sew next Tuesday. Naomi was looking forward to learning. She was determined to be a good wife.

The only other thing she had to do was to make sure they consummated the marriage. At the rate they were going, it may be harder to do if he left the cabin each time they kissed.

Naomi glanced in the small mirror beside the door. Her hair was messy so she pushed the strands back out of her face. Her cheeks were pink, probably from the excitement of the day.

She was so busy staring at herself she never heard him come back in until a shadow fell over her. She peered in the mirror to find him behind her. "You look perfect," he mentioned.

She smiled, quickly turning to him. "I want to look perfect for you."

He took her chin in his two fingers and lifted her face closer. "You are perfect."

She sucked in a breath, glad he was paying attention to her once again. She had to know that he'd never push her away or send her back. Her arms flew around his neck and she pushed her mouth to his in a bold move.

His arms went around her as he deepened the kiss. *Oh my, sweetness! Maybe he does want to kiss me after all!* As he held her closer a loud knock had Russell stepping back again, although it wasn't his fault. He raised and brow and sighed. "I believe my brother is here to welcome us home."

It was not a good time for family, his eyes said, but he let her go and went to the door anyway. Flinging it open, a man the same size as Russell stood there, a grin on his face.

"Congrats, brother!" He stepped inside without being invited and slapped Russell on the shoulder.

When he turned to Naomi, she cried out. The man looked exactly like Russell.

He came towards her, holding out his hand. "Welcome to the family. I'm Wesley and the only way to tell us apart is -"

"The eyes," she finished.

He stopped in his tracks. "Excellent. Mine are blue while Russells are dark brown."

"Almost black," she told him, taking his hand.

"Right." He let her hand go then placed a small, friendly kiss on her cheek. "I'm so happy to meet you."

"Likewise," she told him. "Although we missed you at the wedding." She tried to raise her chin in the air but instead bumped the wall behind her. Trying to act sophisticated was a lot of work!

Wesley made a face. "You alright, there?"

She stepped away from the wall. "Of course."

"Then you won't want to miss Ma's delicious food and a cake the other ladies baked. We're heading up to the White Ranch where a reception is being held in your honor."

"Oh!" She turned to her husband. She remembered Miss Addie mentioning a reception. Russells kisses had made her forget.

"It's probably a good thing," Russell told her. "That way we can get the introductions out of the way. My Ma and stepmother Nora are dying to meet you." His eyes told her he'd rather be here, alone, with her. Another good sign. Naomi was gaining hope that it would all work out in her favor. They'd go to the reception then come home and consummate the marriage. Then she'd be safe and never have to leave here, ever again.

She nodded. "OK, let's go then. A pleasure to have met you," she said to Wesley in a haughty voice. She had to at least act as if she were from a higher class.

The three made their way towards the wagon at the front of the farm house. It was a nice sized house with a large front porch that looked cozy and warm.

A woman came out the front door, much younger than Naomi imagined his mother would be. She had already pictured an older woman with a stern face in her mind.

This woman was simply beautiful. She was older, yes, but without the weathered look and saggy skin of an older woman. She had dark hair, the same color as her sons and a lovely complexion that looked well taken care of. As they got closer, she noticed Widow Young's dark eyes, the same color as Russells. The corners had tiny crows feet adorning the edges but it didn't take from her beauty. If anything, those tiny crows feet enhanced her lovely features.

She gave Naomi a genuine hug. "Welcome. May I call you Naomi?"

Naomi blinked, a bit shaken at the soft, welcoming voice. "Yes, certainly. Thank you, Mrs. Young."

"It's nice to meet you, at last. Well, come along, we have a wonderful reception to attend." Mrs. Young led her to the wagon. She squeezed Naomi's hand before the horse and cart took off across the field towards the large ranch next door.

Naomi didn't know what to think. Her head was reeling, she was almost in tears at the warmth that eluded from Mrs. Young and even Russell's twin brother, Wesley. They didn't stare at her, or lift their noses in the air. No, they welcomed her as if she were part of a family.

Her new family.

As the wagon wheels hit every rut as they crossed the field, it bounced her around a bit. Russell sat beside her, an arm lounging across her shoulder. Now he pulled her closer to keep her from bouncing all over the place.

"Thanks," she whispered, looking up at him. He seemed at peace here on his land. It was quiet and far removed from the noise of any city or town. Even though the wagon still made clacking noises, the beauty of the land combined with the serenity of the landscape seemed perfect.

Naomi watched in genuine interest as the freshly painted gate that separated two properties was opened by an older man, bits of bright red hair sticking out from a weathered hat. He saluted the wagon and shut the gate when they were through. The man climbed on a horse standing by and followed them to the yard where the reception was being held.

Russell ran his hand along her arm, giving her little goosebumps on her flesh. She was quite surprised at all the hospitality. It made her wonder how she was going to pull off acting high-faluting with a crowd like this.

A sigh escaped her.

"You okay with all this, Naomi," Russell asked.

When he spoke, Wesley and Mrs. Young faced her.

She had to say yes even though she was so overwhelmed. She'd rather spend a quiet night enjoying the cabin and being alone with her new husband but this was so joyfully wonderful.

Naomi was unable to speak. She nodded instead.

When a lone tear fell from her cheek, Mrs. Young smiled. "It's a lot to take in, I know. As family, we wanted to make sure you feel welcome."

Russell handed her a handkerchief from his pocket.

She gave him a smile while she wiped the wetness from her face, gathering herself together. "Well, then, let's get on with it, shall we?"

Russell helped her from the wagon. They followed the Widow to the center of the yard where several tables were decked out with many dishes and even offerings from the other farms in the area. Whenever something like this took place, everyone brought a favorite dish, Russell explained to her. All the food made her stomach growl. Naomi was hungry. She wanted to devour the food but thought better of it for now.

There would be time enough to eat. She had to remember to eat like a lady. Feeling her pockets, which were large enough, she thought perhaps she'd stash some food away, in case.

It was a hard habit to break. Of course she wouldn't have to hide food in case there wasn't any for tomorrow! She was home now with a husband and a place where food seemed abundant.

"Welcome, Mrs. Young."

At first, Naomi didn't answer until she realized the older woman was talking to her. She shook her head, not used to being called by someone else's name. This will take some time, she thought to herself.

A tall woman with beautiful thick hair stood alongside the man who opened the gate for them. She gave a quick smile, hoping to get introductions out of the way so they were able to eat.

"Hello."

"I'm Nora and this is my husband Rusty. May I call you Naomi?"

"Of course, I'd prefer it, actually."

"Well, then, Naomi it is. Enjoy the food and the music. Welcome to the family."

Naomi was afraid she was going to shed more tears. Before she did, three women near her age welcomed her.

Melody, Abigail and Callie were married to Nora's sons. They gathered around, shielding Naomi from everyone and led her away from her husband. She looked back a few times to find him conversing with other men. When the men went to the barn, she lost sight of him.

Callie spoke up. She was the friendliest one there. "Naomi, we want you to know if you need anything, anything at all, we are a stone's throw away and can be at your cabin in a wink."

"Thank you, I appreciate including me in. I'm afraid I know nothing about country living. I was raised in the city and we had others to do the chores." She dreaded the lies the moment they came out her mouth but she needed everyone to believe she was well off.

"Is that a fact?" Callie asked.

A moment of silence stood between them as the others watched. Callie was the most outspoken of the three. Naomi wondered how long she'd be able to keep the ruse going? Callie seemed smart. Perhaps she'd have to stay to herself more. If she had to keep to herself, having a cabin like the one Russell had was well worth it.

It was home.

She never, ever had a home of her own. Naomi promised herself she was going to work hard. She was dying to get started actually. But where was Russell? Was he still in the barn with the other men?

When Callie noticed Naomi's eyes kept darting to the barn, she laughed. "Oh, Naomi, the men will be awhile. Come along, we'll introduce you to some of the other townsfolk. They rode out from Wichita Falls and others rode from Mill Ridge to meet Russell's bride."

Naomi longed to be with her husband. Even though she was lying to him he was the only one she felt most at ease with. Plus, she wanted to consummate the marriage so their lives would be sealed and no one would ever make her leave here.

She took one last look back before following the ladies. It was going to be a long night until he was once again by her side.

Naomi didn't want to act haughty, she'd rather embrace everyone and kiss their cheeks like they were doing to her. But she had lied from the beginning, now she had to play her part and act like someone she wasn't.

This was one of the hardest things she'd ever done. As an orphan, there was no one to answer to. No one told you what to do or what to say.

She looked around, watching everyone mingle with smiles and laughter all around. She may have to pretend to be someone she wasn't but it was all worth it. Look at what she had now!

<h1 style="text-align:center">Chapter 4</h1>

Russell stood leaning against the barn door with his brother and half-brothers, watching the crowd as they laughed, talked and ate. Then Luke and Adam parted ways to find their wives and Samuel went to help Callie and Nora clear the tables. He longed to find his wife and take her home except she seemed to be missing.

"There she is," Wesley pointed.

"Where?"

"She's partially hidden behind the large oak tree. She didn't seem at all shy when I met her, wonder why she is trying to hide?" Wesley asked.

"Not sure. She was enjoying herself with the ladies earlier. I suppose this is a lot to take in, brother." He pushed himself away from the side of the barn. " I'm going to take my bride home."

The fading sun was starting to lower in the sky. Russell made his way through the thinning crowd, most of them packing up to head back to their homesteads. The sound of the fiddle rent the air as Rusty began playing. A small camp-fire glowed nearby.

He stopped for a moment to stare at his bride. She was beautiful. Her eyes glowed. They were bright and filled with wonder.

When they had first met she seemed scared, tense. Russell imagined the fear of traveling from her home to a strange place and starting over was enough to scare anyone. Now, she was leaning against the tree, contentment in her eyes. For now she was content. He wondered if it was enough to keep her happy.

She was from a well to do family, used to having things handed to her. Here, the farm was a whole different world. There were chores to do and lots of work had by everyone, including her. How was she going to react when she realized her job in the mornings was to go outside to the chicken coop to gather eggs no matter what kind of weather?

She happened to look at him just as he began to take another step towards her. Her eyes lit up. A smile played across her mouth. She seemed happy to see him.

He wanted to kiss her. Russell ran a hand through his hair. She was beautiful. "Hello, Mrs. Young."

She took his hand in hers. He liked how bold she was, not afraid to show affection. "I missed you," she told him.

He kissed her hand before gazing into those velvety blue eyes. "We should go," he told her.

She nodded. "I'm ready. It's been a long day."

When he raised a brow, she sucked in her breath. "I'm sorry," she told him, placing a hand on his chest.

Her touch made him aware there was more to their wedding night if he so desired. "What are you sorry for?"

"When I said it's been a long day, I hope you didn't take offense. I've traveled far and it's been quite the adventure today."

She was right. Today was their wedding day but she was exhausted from a long trip and vulnerable and he wasn't about to take advantage of her. No, he'd take her home and leave her be. They had plenty of time to consummate this marriage.

And they would, one way or another. Just not tonight. He wanted no regrets.

Russell had to do everything in his power to make sure she was willing to stay by his side. Now that he realized how much he wanted her as a permanent wife, the thought of the thirty day trial period frustrated him even more. He had thirty days to make her his own.

He wasn't sure his small cabin on the farm was enough to keep her by his side. According to the letter she wrote, Naomi was used to sophistication, city-dwellers that probably wore fancy suits, courting her at fancy restaurants and special places in the big city. How was he going to compete with that?

After they said their goodbyes, the trip back to the cabin was relatively quiet. There was a half-moon tonight while the path home was lit by the brilliant light of a thousand tiny, shining stars. It seemed perfect for a wedding night.

Too perfect. Except for one thing. When Russell stopped the buggy, he placed his wife in his arms. Her head lolled to one side. She had fallen asleep on the ride home and he didn't have the heart to wake her.

Russell had enjoyed the feel of her against him while she slept. At first he had wanted to stop the buggy and take her in his arms but when he looked over and noticed she had fallen asleep, he realized how much more he wanted to be her protector.

And how serene and beautiful she was.

He wanted to make her his bride in every way.

<><>

A sliver of sunshine peeked in through the small window. At first Naomi forgot where she was. She stretched, her arms above her head, enjoying the feel of softness underneath. Her fingers touched the wooden bed post. It almost scared her at first. She thought she was back at the orphanage except the bed rails on those beds were made of iron.

They also had lumpy, awful mattresses that smelled. The one she was lying on was so soft she didn't want to get up and it certainly didn't smell bad. Looking around, Naomi realized she was alone in a bedroom, a soft quilt covering her. She was still dressed in yesterday's clothes except for her boots, which were placed side by side on the wood planked floor.

Had Russell carried her to bed? She remembered sitting on the seat next to him in the buggy as they made their way towards the cabin. She remembered his soft shoulder when her head found it on the ride home. Then she woke up here and now. She was almost embarrassed that she fell asleep on him.

He was such a gentleman. It was his right to consummate the marriage and she almost wished he had, that way she'd never have to leave here again. But he didn't. Instead, he had treated her kindly, being gentle with her, letting her sleep, like a man who seemed to care.

Or, was the truth of the matter that he really didn't want her as a wife? Was he bidding his time for the next thirty days until he could send her back? Was that why he had left her sleep?

Frustrated, Naomi got out of bed, not sure of the answer. She splashed water on her face and washed up the best she could, refreshing her skirts and putting on her shoes. It was time to find her husband and get some answers. If he wanted her gone, then he needed to tell her. She would rather leave now, go back to the city before she fell any more in love with this farm.

He was in the other room making fresh eggs on the cook stove. Surprised, she stopped to watch him. Russell wielded the pan like he was familiar with the task. Which was actually a good thing.

Naomi had no idea how to cook. She'd never used a cook stove, let alone one of those iron pans he was working out of. He waited while the lard heated up then placed an egg in the palm of his hand. With a quick snap of his wrist, he cracked the egg on the side of the pan and let it dribble into the lard.

She crossed her arms over her waist, watching, her head tilted to one side. It looked relatively simple.

"Good morning," Russell said, his eyes on the pan of eggs. "If you'll have a seat at my table, I am about to serve the best eggs this side of the Rio Grande."

Naomi suddenly noticed two settings at the small table that sat against the wall of the cabin. She took a seat, propping her elbow on the table until realizing a lady didn't sit like an urchin. She removed her arm but drummed her fingers against the table top, slightly nervous being alone with him.

Russell glanced over at her, grinning. "I'm not very good at cooking as you will see, except for eggs. I can make eggs all day long."

"It's kind of you to do so. I believe I slept in," she told him, annoyed at herself for not getting up earlier. He probably got tired of waiting for her to wake up, she mused.

"I'm glad you did. Today we'll enjoy breakfast and I'll show you around the farm."

He filled both their plates, along with a slice of bread smothered with creamy butter. When he sat down, he took her hand, bowing his head and lifting them both in prayer. Naomi peeked at him as he said grace, amazed. Would life be like this every single morning?

When he lifted his head, Russell caught her staring. She looked away, embarrassed. He still held her hand for another moment. "Dig in! What are you waiting for!"

She did. Boy, did she ever. The smell of eggs had drifted up her nose the whole time he was praying and she was famished. She had never woke up to a hot meal like this before. Not in all of her years as an orphan. Not even when she lived in St. Catherine's Orphanage for that short period of time. There, she had tons of chores to do before they ate a breakfast of porridge and hard, day old bread.

Naomi leaned her head down and shoveled the food in her mouth, forgetting she was at the table with her new husband. She moaned with each bite, closing her eyes and lifting her face to the sky. After she sopped the egg with her bread, she finished it off and wiped her mouth, sitting back against the chair. She was in pure, blissfull heaven.

Naomi sighed.

"I'm glad you enjoyed breakfast."

Her eyes flew open. "Oh dear, I'm sorry! The smell was so enticing. I am embarrassed." He probably thinks she is out of her mind! Her face burned crimson as she felt the heat rising from the middle of her neck to her cheeks. How in the world had she forgotten he was right across the table from her?

"If I didn't know better, you'd think it was the first time you ate eggs."

She waved him off, racking her brain to come up with an intelligent answer. "To be honest, I had not been eating properly since I left home. This is the first meal I've enjoyed for weeks."

"You certainly enjoyed it, which makes me happy."

She stood up, wanting to do something to get away from the amused look on his face. If he knew she was an orphan, living on the streets and scrounging for food day after day, he'd no doubt send her back on the next train.

Especially after she lied and said she was from a well-to-do family. She had to start acting like it now before she made too many obvious mistakes. One mistake was bad, but this had to stop before she got caught. She wanted to be honest and tell him, and every time she thought she was brave enough to, something always stopped her from saying the words. So she lied even more to keep up the farce.

"I'm afraid we had servants at home so I'm not too familiar with cooking and cleaning. I'm willing to learn, unless you want to hire a servant?"

Russell collected the plates. He turned to her. "I can't afford a servant. I'm sure Ma will help teach you what needs done and I'll take you around, show you some chores that will help here. She has had to do everything on her own for so many years. It'll be a big help if you can take over a few things."

Did he sound disappointed? "I'll do my best," she told him, silently promising to learn everything so he would be proud of her and keep her. She had thirty days to learn how to be a good wife and vowed not to spill her secret no matter what. He needed a helper for his Ma and so be it, she was going to do her best.

He placed the plates in a pan of water and turned to her. Placing both hands on her shoulders, he drew her to him, placing a kiss on her forehead. "I hope you can get used to this kind of life. I know your family has had hired help but I'm a farmer. There is no way to provide the kind of life you were used to. Are you sure you want this?"

Was he worried she couldn't be happy here? She had to convince him there was no need to worry. She placed her hands on his cheeks, drawing him closer. "I want to learn everything about being a farmer's wife. Even if it means having to get my hands dirty. You won't be sorry you married me." Now she felt even worse for lying to him about where she came from. Naomi ached to blurt out the truth.

She kept going back and forth, one minute wanting to tell him, the next moment vowing to be silent. Before things got too out of hand, perhaps she needed to be honest. All of her hopes and dreams may die within the next few moments but he deserved honesty. This was so hard but he was a good man. "There's something I want to tell you."

Her words were interrupted by a loud shotgun blast. Naomi jumped three feet in the air, almost toppling over.

Russell went to the front door, grabbing the rifle setting upright against the wall. "Stay here," he told her. "There's another rifle in the bedroom if you need it. Do you know how to shoot?"

She didn't get a chance to answer him when another blast went off. Survival instinct took over. Naomi crouched behind the rocker sitting in the room by the window. Her hands shook. She watched her husband go out the door, his rifle at the ready.

A few minutes later Naomi heard a scuffling noise on the porch. Her husband would speak up, wouldn't he? Then who was there? She was afraid to lift her head. What if it was an outlaw outside? Who was doing the shooting? Fear for her husband sent shivers down her spine. What if he was shot and killed? Her mind was in a confused state. What ifs would not keep her husband safe. Naomi had to help.

She had to make her way to the bedroom for the other rifle even if she didn't know how to shoot. Staying low to the floor, she reached the bedroom where the shotgun was propped up behind the door. Naomi stared at it for a moment, then took hold of the handle and made her way back out to the window, keeping low the whole time.

The wooden floorboards of the porch creaked. More shuffling sounds were heard. She listened, crouching under the window. It sounded like someone was having trouble breathing as short bursts of air fogged up the window. What in the world was out there?

Naomi sucked in a deep, haggard breath and slowly stood up, taking aim, her finger close to the trigger. Squinting through the foggy window, she dropped the rifle to the floor and screamed at the top of her lungs. A big, shaggy black monster with round eyes and fluid dripping from its snout stared through the fog dead at her. She backed away, horrified when it grunted and bellowed at her through the window.

Another shotgun blast had Naomi running for the bedroom. She didn't look back but slid under the bed, petrified. Her whole body shook. Never in her whole life had she seen a creature like that before. In New York, rats the size of cats and small dogs were common but this horned monster was huge!

She wedged herself underneath the mattress, praying to God to keep her safe. Her worst fear was the thing ate her husband! Where was he?

Muffled noises and more shotgun blasts right before it got real quiet. Naomi held her breath, petrified.

It seemed like hours until the wooden door creaked when it opened. Footsteps came across the room. Relief surged through her when his voice called her name. When he knelt down and peered under the bed, her eyes wide and terrified, she was unable to speak.

He reached out his hand. Naomi always thought she was tough. Living on the streets had made her fear little. Or, so she thought. This was a whole new world and she realized in that moment she had no idea of the dangers all over.

"Come out, Naomi. The Bison is dead."

"B-bison?"

He nodded, gently taking hold of her arm and pulling her out. When she stood upright, her knees went to jelly and she began to topple to the floor. He picked her up, sat down on the edge of the bed and placed her on his lap. "He got away from the herd. We tried to run him off but they are unpredictable animals. When I saw him on the porch it was time to take him down."

She was curled up in his arms, her face against his chest. "I've never been so afraid in my life."

Russell ran a hand over her hair. "No need to be scared. I've got you now."

"Thank you." No one had ever come to her rescue. Naomi hadn't known she needed rescuing. She always thought she was able to handle whatever came her way. "I thought the shaggy monster would break through the window."

Russell's brother and mother came through the door, calling out.

"In here, Ma!"

Wesley and Widow Young hurried in to make sure Naomi was safe. "We weren't sure if you had tried to run outside. You sure scared us," Widow Young said, giving her a hug.

Naomi let the tears flow. It was something she never thought she'd do in front of anyone. Why were her emotions all over the place? She was a hardened orphan. Nothing phased her in all the years she was left without a family. She had vowed no one would see her cry or in a weakened state. Now, here she was, being a big baby in front of her new family.

"Now, now, it's all over, Naomi. You should lie down."

Russell lifted her up, placing her on the bed.

Widow Young wet a cloth and placed it on her head before turning to her sons. "Boys, there is an animal to butcher. Rusty heard the shots and is gathering a few hands to help. Go on now, I'll take care of Naomi."

Russell pushed a strand of hair from her face, placing a kiss on her lips. "I'll be back later. You get some rest."

She didn't want to rest but her insides were tossing and turning. She was afraid to move. Widow Young pulled a chair close to the bed. She had a small bowl filled with fresh water, dipping the cloth and placing it back on Naomi's forehead. It did feel soothing.

Naomi closed her eyes. "I am sorry. I didn't mean to be such a coward."

"Nonsense. I'm sure you've never seen a wild animal like that living in the big city."

"Only rats. Homeless cats and dogs, but no creatures like that."

Widow Young stared at her. She felt it even with her eyes closed. "Oh? Why would you know about such things where you lived? I've heard that only happens in the poorest of areas."

Naomi's first mistake! She had been living amongst the squalor of the homeless. Crawling in windows of abandoned or closed buildings to find a warm place to sleep. Begging for food or stealing a muffin now and again off a food cart to fill her rumbling belly. There were plenty of wild cats who scouraged for food just like she did.

There was no end to her lies now. She had to make everyone believe she was a decent, well-bred person. Besides the awful monster, this place was heaven. She didn't want to lose it and have to go back to live in the street ever again. Even though she had wanted to tell the truth, she didn't want to give up this place. Not now, not ever.

So, she continued her lies. "Once a month our cook was allowed to send food out for the homeless. I rode along once and saw the abhorrent way those people lived. When my father found out, he had a fit and ordered me to never do so again. Once was enough." Naomi had been the recipient of the wealthy's food give-aways. Every now and again a carriage would come by the docks, throwing leftovers for the poor. She sometimes hung around the docks for days to be sure to be there for the hand out, stuffing her pockets to make sure she'd have enough to eat for the next few days.

"Well, that was nice of your parents to give to the needy." Widow Young stood. "Let's get you up and about. Are you able to walk?"

"I believe so." Naomi tried to stand, relieved when her legs no longer shook.

Russell's mother turned, hands on her hips. "Now that you are back to normal, follow me," she ordered, her voice stern. "We have a busy day ahead."

"Oh?" What in the world happened to his Ma? The woman was sweet as pie a moment ago.

"The men will be busy all day butchering the bison. It's time you learn how to be a farmer's wife. Come along, we have a lot of work to do."

Did she know Naomi was a fraud? Sheer terror engulfed her whole body, keeping her feet frozen to the floor boards.

When she didn't follow, Widow Young turned and frowned. "Naomi, I know you have been brought up in a well bred family. But that doesn't mean you can neglect work here. Your husband will need you to be able to help keep the place going. I can help you. We have no hired help here. Are you ready to learn?" Her tone was softer. Perhaps Naomi had taken her wrong because of her own guilt. Widow Young was a no-nonsense woman who got things done. She'd better listen to her.

A wave of relief almost knocked her over. Naomi smiled. "I sure am."

# Chapter 5

Several days later, Naomi had learned so much from his mother. She was ready to make bison stew. She had spent the last several afternoons with Widow Young while the older woman taught her a variety of dishes to prepare. Learning how to make bread and churn butter was the most difficult. Next week, his Ma was going to show her how to bake pies.

Everything seemed easy enough when his mother was by her side guiding her in the kitchen. Now, she found herself alone in her own space, a large pot of cut up meat cooking away. Naomi went out to the garden where fresh vegetables were growing in abundance. She picked a variety, then hurried back to the kitchen, trying to recall Widow Youngs instructions as she cleaned off the dirt.

*After the meat boils, place the vegetables in the water and stir.* One by one, Naomi carefully dropped each whole vegetable in the boiling water. The long carrots took up so much space, she hoped they'd shrink somewhat. Large potatoes sunk to the bottom of the pot, eventually making the water boil over onto the stove. Naomi jumped back the first time it sizzled and spilled over.

She emptied all the vegetables in the big pot. They'd have stew for a month of Sundays! She nodded, proud of herself. Wiping her hands on the apron, Naomi peeked under the towel where her bread was rising.

Time to bake it in the oven and set the table. This day was turning out perfect. She busied herself at the table, then ran outside to pick a few bluebonnets in the yard. Taking a small glass, she filled it with water and placed the flowers in the center of the table.

The water boiled over again, splashing onto the cook stove. Naomi smiled as she wiped it up, not too worried about the mess she made. When she went to stir the pot, the potatoes were losing their skins, falling off into the water, giving the stew water a muddy look. It didn't look like that when Widow Young made stew a few days ago. There was something she forgot to do but her mind was reeling as she tried to remember everything.

Naomi gritted her teeth and hoped for the best. It was time to bake the bread, so she uncovered the pan and set it in the oven on the small rack inside. Closing the door, she turned the knob to keep the door closed and the heat in.

Naomi looked around the room, proud of her accomplishments. The table was set, now all she had to do was make some fresh lemonade. A bowl sat on the counter, so she did like Widow Young showed her and squeezed the juice into a small pitcher and added more water. She rummaged around on the shelves, trying to remember what else to put in the lemonade. Ah, sugar!

There was no sugar to be found anywhere. There was, however, some flour, which apparently was used in the same way. Naomi took a few tablespoons full and dumped them in the pitcher. Except the flour clumped more than dissolved. Oh, dear!

"I wonder why it won't work for me?" She stirred for over ten minutes, then satisfied, poured two glasses. The white clumps sank to the bottom of the glass. She was pretty sure Russell would notice those ugly clumps. So, she quickly poured the lemonade back in the pitcher and found two tin cups instead that were not see through. There, now the flour clumps were hidden from sight.

After stirring the pot again, Naomi noticed the juices had cooked down or either boiled over. She wasn't honestly sure which. It was so darn thick she wondered if perhaps more water would thin it out. Then she heard Russell's steps on the porch and forgot about thinning the stew as excitement ran through every vein in her body. He was going to get his first taste of her cooking supper all by herself.

Maybe he'd even want to consummate their marriage after tonight!

"My, you've been busy." Russell hung his hat on the hook on the wall while closing the door behind him. He turned and gave her a big smile.

Her heart leapt in to her throat as she saw how pleased he looked.

"Yes, I have," Naomi said. "Why don't you have a seat at the table and we'll eat. I'm sure you are hungry." When he took off his hat, a clump of hair hung over his forehead. Naomi went up to him and brushed it back. "I'm glad you're home."

Home. She never would get used to saying that word. She went to turn when a hand shot out. He turned her around and placed a quick kiss on her cheek.

Without a word, he sat down at the table, grinning.

She was grinning, too. This felt nice. Right. As if she belonged here in this home. With Russell.

He coughed.

She giggled.

He handed her a plate.

Her face began to heat up. "Oh, I'm sorry." Taking the plate, Naomi used a ladle to scoop up a thick spoonful of stew. It was dark looking, more so than Widow Young's stew but she was certain it was delicious.

Before setting down his plate, a thought occurred. Maybe she should've tasted the stew before serving.

Yet, it smelled fine, so she went ahead and set the plate in front of him, then took her own plate and filled it with a scoop of stew. She didn't plan to eat much, she was much too nervous.

When she realized the bread hadn't been taken out, her heart sank, afraid it was ruined. Jumping up from the table, Naomi quickly grabbed a towel and pulled open the door.

A sense of relief went through her. The bread looked delicious. She set it on the table beside the bowl of whipped butter. "Well have to let it cool off a few minutes before we cut a slice."

Sitting back down, she reached over to take Russell's hand as he said Grace. When finished, he stared at the food, a look of shock rendered on his face that he quickly tried to hide. His brow rose and he gave her a puzzled look. "Where was Ma today?" he asked, his voice sounding uncertain.

Naomi patted his hand and sat back. "She went to Cooper's Ridge earlier today but I told her not to worry, I had the whole stew recipe down pat. Go on, taste it and tell me what you think."

She heard the intake of air as he took in a deep breath. Russell hesitated a moment before he picked up the fork beside his plate. Watching in anticipation, her nerves were on edge. Would he like her first supper?

Her hands were clasped together on the table. He stared at her hands for a moment and then the stew on his plate. Finally, Naomi let out a breath when he took a forkful of stew in his mouth.

Her face fell when a strangling noise rose up from his throat. Even though he tried hard to hide his distaste, she knew in an instant he didn't like it.

Her hand went to her throat. "I'm so sorry."

Russell waved his hands in front of him. Trying to speak, he mumbled then pointed to the glass of lemonade by his plate.

She reached for the tumbler, handing it to him, concerned. Why wasn't he able to speak?

Sweat poured from Russell's brow. He gulped the lemonade and then pushed his chair back and stood straight up, eyes wide before he ran outside. She thought the words excuse me escaped from his throat but she was too upset to listen.

Her supper wasn't that bad, was it? She scooped a forkful in to her mouth and gagged at the taste. The salt was overpowering, potatoes tasted pasty, making her gag like he did a moment ago.

She took the tin cup to her mouth, drinking lemonade to get the pasty, salty taste from her mouth. Clumps of flour floated around in the liquid and some got in her mouth, which made it even worse.

Naomi ran for the front door, out onto the porch where she hung her head over the railing and spit out the awful food! It had almost made her throw up.

Russell came up beside her, wiping his mouth with the back of his hand. He reached in his pocket and handed her a hanky.

"Thanks," she mumbled, completely embarrassed.

Then he did something she never expected. A laugh rumbled deep in his gut and came out loud and clear. He flung his head back and roared with laughter.

She looked at him, shocked, not sure whether to laugh or cry. Then, a smile spread across her face as she joined him, holding her belly and almost doubling over.

They wound up sitting on the bench outside, gazing at the way the sun was starting to fade into the horizon. Russell took her hand in his. "I am sorry your first meal didn't turn out well."

She shrugged. "I am, too. I'm sorry."

"No need to be. I guess having your own servants to do everything does make it difficult to go out on your own. I'm sure Ma will help you again."

"I thought I was ready. Clearly, I was wrong. What am I going to do with that giant pot of stew?"

Russell smiled. "I'm not even sure. Ask Ma, she'll help you figure it out. Perhaps some of the animals here or at the White Ranch can eat it. In the meantime, are you hungry?"

"A little. You?"

He nodded. "Sure am. I tell you what. You go on an clean up the kitchen and I'll run to Ma's and borrow two bowls of her supper. It should be simmering on her stove. Even if she goes away, supper is always made."

"Are you sure?"

He leaned over and kissed her on the cheek. "Sure as I'll ever be. Go on now, I'll be right back."

Naomi rose up, excited and relieved he wasn't mad. "I did make some fresh bread and it looks and smells wonderful. I'm pretty sure it tastes as good as it looks." At least there was one thing she was able to do right.

"Good. Good, then. I'll be right back."

While Russell was across the yard at his Ma's getting food, Naomi came up with an idea. She cleared off the small kitchen table and drug it outside on to the small porch. Then she brought out the two chairs, found a sheet and placed it over the top of the table. Placing the vase of bluebonnets and a small oil lamp in the center, she went inside to slice the bread.

Taking a small nibble, she nodded in approval. It didn't have too much of any one ingredient, no powerful smell or taste, so she was in the clear. He thought she never worked at a stove before because she was a wealthy socialite and had servants to do their bidding.

If he only knew!

She could straighten this all out if she told him the truth. Something deep down told her he was an understanding man and would care for her even if she had lied. Yet, in just three more weeks the thirty days were up. She didn't want to take any chances he'd get mad and send her packing.

No. Not yet. She had to be sure. After the thirty days, then she'd be honest. Maybe. It would be too late and he'd be stuck with her. Was that wrong?

Naomi loved it here. She loved his family. She loved him. Oh, dear! How can she love a man so quickly? His touch, his intent gaze when he looked at her, it was so surreal. He seemed to care, at least a little. Maybe that was all she'd ever need.

Naomi went outside to sit at the table and wait on Russell to return. She placed the plate of bread there, covered with a towel and a bowl of whipped butter. Taking her finger, she dipped it into the butter and tasted to make sure there would be no more surprises.

Russell soon returned with a pot of his Ma's chicken and dumplings. After getting them both a bowl, he sat in the space across from her, a content smile on his face. "This is nice."

"Thank you. I thought it would be nice to watch the sun go down while we eat."

Russell lowered his head, taking her hand without looking as if he knew where to find it and began Grace. "Thank you, Lord. For everything. For my home, wife and family. We may not always be perfect but that job is for you, not us. Amen."

"Amen."

<><>

Russell enjoyed their supper on the porch. It was a sweet idea. Naomi was trying to make it up to him and he was pleased. She was trying to be such a good wife. His expectations were high because his Ma made things like cooking and taking care of a homestead easy. She had done it alone for so long.

Naomi had so much to learn. Thank the good Lord his Ma was next door while she experimented with food.

"What are you thinking about?"

Her soft voice cut into his thoughts.

He reached across the table and took her hand. "I'm thinking about you."

"Oh, goodness, me! Whatever for?"

She almost looked afraid when he said that to her. It made him smile. "You've changed your whole life to marry a farmer. I'll be surprised if you want to stick around after our thirty day trial."

She shook her head back and forth. "Oh, Russell. I want to stay. I am afraid you will send me away."

He was perplexed. "Why in the world would I send you away? I've got the golden egg, so to speak. A wonderful lady from a well bred family like yours makes me the luckiest farmer in the world. The other ranches and farms from miles away are so envious of what I have right now."

"Are you saying you are glad I'm from a wealthy family and not from some poor family?"

He chuckled, rubbing his fingers over her hand, which moments ago was soft and plush in his. Now, her fingers were stiff and she was trying to pull away. He held onto her hand anyway, ready to tell her he didn't care if she were rich or poor.

Just then, she pulled away, pushing her chair back and gathering their plates. "It's time to clear the table," she mumbled, taking the dishes inside, not looking at him.

Russell stood, confused. She seemed rather upset and in a big hurry all of a sudden. What had happened to their evening? He propped open the door to drag the table back in, along with the chairs. Glancing at Naomi, she busied herself with cleaning the dishes.

When he was done, he stood behind her, wanting to take her in his arms but she seemed distant all of a sudden. He wasn't sure how to proceed. "Naomi, is everything okay?"

She didn't turn around when he stepped closer. "Fine. I'm tired, it's been such a long day. I'll finish these up and then say goodnight."

"It's getting harder to sleep on the floor. I'd like to sleep in the bed if you don't mind."

He was hoping she would say yes. It was about time to get this consummation over with and she became his wife in everything besides just his name. Unless she was not willing. Then he'd wait.

"I. I am not sure I'm ready for, oh, you know."

Russell took a step closer. He brushed his knuckles across her cheek, lowering his mouth to her ear. "I'm more than ready," he told her, hoping she'd want to also. He needed to know she would stay when the time was up. He was afraid when she became quiet like this, as if she were planning to change her mind.

"I'm a terrible cook," she said, not looking at him.

He was so close to her, taking in the smell of roses that drifted from her skin. He smiled when he noticed speckles of flour in her hair. She had been working hard to please him even if the food was bad. "You will learn. One bad meal isn't the end of things. Come on, lets lock up and go to bed."

Russell wanted a real marriage. Not one where he had a choice in thirty days. Yes, at first he wanted to do everything in his power so he didn't have to go through with it, but not any more. Now, he wanted Naomi with him forever. He wanted her by his side through whatever storms and tribulations they went through.

He was in love.

It was too soon to be in love. Wasn't it?

A banging on the door caused Naomi to jump. She spun around, her eyes wide. "Who would be at the door this time of night?"

"I don't know. Stay here. I'll check."

Russell let his twin brother in. "What's wrong, Wesley?" The look on his brothers face was filled with worry.

"It's Ma. She was coming back from Coopers Ridge and something spooked the horse. Her buggy overturned, trapping one of Ma's legs underneath."

Russell's heart almost stopped. He didn't have time to waste. Whipping his hat from the peg on the wall, he turned to Naomi. "I'm sorry, I have to go."

Naomi rapped her arms around his neck, pressing her lips to his. "Be careful. I'll be here when you get back. Let me know if there is anything I can do."

Russell figured it would be better if she went to the main house. "If you can go to Ma's place and get her bed ready it will be a big help. I'm sure she can use a cup of hot coffee when we get her home."

"I'll go now."

He turned to give her one more kiss before he went out the door. "Thanks."

She smiled, yet it didn't reach her eyes. Naomi cared for his Ma and he saw the worry in her eyes.

Outside, Wesley had both horses ready and waiting. "Where to, Wes?"

"Up the road about two miles. Some of Rusty's men are headed there now. He said she was going too fast for the turn and the horse lost its footing around the bend. Doesn't sound like Ma, she knows how to handle that buggy."

The two rode hell-bent for leather until they came upon the crash scene. The horse was a bit shook up, but the buggy was almost on it's roof. The men who made it there first had pulled her free from the wreckage.

A large surge of relief went through Russell when he saw her leg intact. Out here, on the prairie, it was hard to find a doctor unless they rode to Wichita Falls or Mill Ridge. Russell would ride all night if he had to if Ma needed medical help.

"Ma?" Russell kneeled by her side. "You hurting?"

She nodded, her face pale. "My foot. Help me up, boys. These men wouldn't let me up until you showed up. Now, let's go home."

Russell picked her up from the ground where she was half-sitting. She was not steady on her feet and when she tried to take a step with her injured leg, she cried out in pain. "I guess it is a bit sore." She gritted her teeth.

"That's enough." Russell picked her up and carried her to the wagon Rusty had waiting. "Thanks, neighbor," he told the old man.

"No problem. Let's get her back to the farm."

Rusty drove the wagon carefully, trying to avoid major ruts in the road. Russell was grateful the old man knew to try not to jar her leg any more than necessary. His Ma moaned every now and again but she was tough. He wished she had a partner for times like this but she never bothered courting anyone else. In the meantime, him and Wesley would take care of her.

Now it was her turn to be cared for. To Russell's relief the lights were on at the farm house. Oil lamps burned, shining their light through the downstairs window. He was glad his Ma's room was on the first floor since she may be out of commission for awhile.

He picked her up and carried her inside while Naomi guided them to the bedroom, pulling down the blankets. "Widow Young, I have some coffee for you."

Without waiting for an answer, she left to fetch the cup of coffee. Russell watched as she busied herself in the kitchen. He stood at the door to his Ma's room, standing back while Rusty and Norah White were checking Ma's leg. "How is she?" he asked.

"Looks like a bad bruise or sprain, nothing seems broken," Rusty murmured.

Nora spoke up, propping a few pillows and placing them under his Ma's head. "Now you listen good. I've sent for Doc James in Wichita Falls. I'm sure him and Nurse Ellie will head out first thing in the morning. Rusty is going to wrap your leg but I want you to promise me you will not get out of bed until the doc sees you."

"But, there's so much to do. I can't stop working for a little sore foot." Widow Young tried to sit up.

"Nonsense," Nora told her, shaking a finger at his Ma.

"She's right," his wife interrupted, carrying a cup of coffee on a saucer. She placed it in his Ma's hands. "No pressure on the foot until the doctor arrives. Your sons and I will make sure you don't do any more damage."

He was so proud of his wife in that moment. She stood above his mother, looking a bit frightened and yet when she placed her hands on her hips and stuck that cute little chin in the air, he wanted to pull her against him and kiss her.

She was taking charge and his Ma even nodded and took a sip of her coffee.

Nora smiled in the background.

Russell grinned.

Until his wife's chin went up in the air a bit too far. She tried to step away but tripped over herself. She stumbled and dropped out of sight.

The other ladies in the room gasped.

Naomi's head popped back up. She stood, brushed off her skirts and gave an awkward smile. "I'm alright. I'll be right outside if you need me." She walked out of the room, her chin not quite so far in the air this time.

Russell crossed his arms over his chest, amused, yet curious. For being raised in a wealthy family, she sure wasn't very steady on her feet. Didn't they go to some type of school to learn how to be ladies and act proper?

She sure surprised him.

He leaned back against the door frame.

It was going to be an interesting marriage. He had wanted to consummate it tonight but that wasn't going to happen. Hopefully, soon. He didn't want to lose her.

# Chapter 6

She peered in the mirror by the front door to see how red her cheeks were. Patting them down made her feel as if she were making the embarrassment fade. Every single time she tried to act sophisticated, she wound up hitting her head against something or she'd wind up on the floor.

High society wasn't for her. She needed to tell him she was a nobody. An orphan. Staring at herself in the mirror, a frown appeared. Now wasn't the time to be selfish and think about her past.

Widow Young needed her. Her mind made up, she would help take care of Russell's Ma and then figure out her next move. In the meantime, perhaps her stance on consummating the marriage was changing.

How can she ask him to live the rest of his life with a liar and a cheat? She was cheating him of a lady born of a better class than her. Why hadn't she seen the truth. An orphan belonged on the streets. Not in a home like this with such loving, kind people.

Naomi didn't deserve a life like this one. A life like this was never meant for her. It was meant for someone else.

The realization made her sick in the stomach. Tears welled up in her eyes. She excused herself when Wesley came through the front door. "I'll be right back," she mumbled then fled to their cabin across the yard. She needed time to get herself together. Russell cannot see her cry.

Naomi spent the better part of ten minutes feeling sorry for herself. Wiping the tears from her eyes, she left the bedroom with a change of clothing. Looking around the cabin, she was determined to stay with Widow Young while she figured out her next move. The longer she stayed in this cabin with her husband, the less likely she'd be able to leave in thirty days.

She would not be the one to condemn him to a life with an unworthy woman. She was tired of going back and forth, one minute thinking she'd tell him the truth, the next moment trying to hide the truth. Sooner or later, she'd be found out and then what? She was a selfish person wanting more than she deserved.

Naomi made sure the tell-tale sign of tears were no longer on her cheeks. She made her way back to the big house and got busy in the kitchen. There were a few dishes to wash up and the floor needed sweeping. At least she knew how to sweep a floor.

Nora said goodnight as her and Rusty left. That left her alone with Wesley and Russell. Both boys were sitting in with their Ma. It was time they got some rest. Naomi took a deep breath.

"It's time for you two to let your Ma get some rest."

"I don't plan to leave her alone," Russell told Naomi.

"You won't have to. I was at the cabin for a change of clothes and plan to spend the night here in the rocker by her bedside. You go on, if anything changes, I'll call for you. I'll stay here with her for as long as I need to be." Until I leave, she thought, not saying those words out loud. A sadness rippled through her soul.

Wesley stood. "Thank you, Naomi. You're right. There's always work to do. I'm going up to bed. Ma, you tell Naomi if you need us. I love you." He kissed his Ma on the cheek. She had been dozing off and smiled weakly.

Naomi nudged Russell. "You, too. I'll be fine here."

He stood, stretched and stared at her, all in one sleek move. "You sure that's why you want to stay here?"

"Of course it is, your Ma needs cared for." He suspected she didn't want to be alone with him. *Please don't make this difficult! I don't have a plan yet!*

Russell nodded and kissed her on the forehead. "Goodnight, Naomi. I'll go get a few hours sleep and be back to check on everyone."

She didn't argue, knowing he'd be back first thing in the morning. At least she was here, safe from his advances. Yet, she wanted his advances so much. Let's face it, she never got what she wanted. Hers was a life she hadn't asked for. Ironically, she got a taste of the good life but that's all it was, a tease.

A deep sigh escaped Naomi as she sat down by Ma's bedside. She took a small Afghan and covered her lap, a feeling of defeat and dread overwhelming her.

Naomi had fallen asleep in the chair. She sensed someone watching her but didn't want to open her eyes yet knowing it was Russell. With her eyes closed, she imagined him leaning against the doorway, his dark eyes on her while she slept.

It almost made her cry out. When he finds out her plans to leave, he'd never look at her again. He'd be angry and hurt, she knew, but it couldn't be helped. He deserved more.

At least she should try to make use of her time while here. Stirring, she opened her eyes and gave him a smile. He had been watching her with such an intense look it surprised Naomi.

He had to stop this! The way he looked at her made her falter. Made her rethink all of her decisions.

"Good morning, Russell. Your mother is still asleep but I can make some coffee." At least she was able to do that well.

"No need, I've already made some. Come outside with me and have a cup."

She didn't want to go anywhere with him. Being alone would only make things worse. Yet, she had no choice, she didn't want to wake up Widow Young. Nodding, she got up and left the bedroom, pouring herself a cup of coffee and avoiding his gaze.

Outside, they sat in the two rockers on the porch. There was still dew on the ground, patches of fog here and there covering the prairie. The sun hadn't come up yet, it was hiding behind some clouds. It didn't look as if it were going to be a nice day.

Her heart was in her throat. Russell had no clue she was about to tell him her plans to leave. She had to wait until his mother recovered but it was so hard to act normal. Whatever normal was.

He took her free hand in his. "I love watching the sun come up. Mostly, I'm in the barn with Dolly this time of morning but I wanted to stop and see how you were doing."

"You mean how your Ma is doing?"

"No, I mean you. It was hard to sleep last night knowing you weren't there."

She was shocked. They hadn't known each other long at all and he missed her presence already? Wasn't this all moving too fast? How was she going to break the news to him when he kept saying and doing things like this?

She decided to change the subject and not acknowledge his words. Somewhere in the Ladies Gazette it said it is better to say too little than too much.

She was grateful when a buggy came barrelling down the driveway, leaving a cloud of dust in the air. "It must be the doc," she said, setting her cup on the table beside the rocker and standing up.

"It's Doc James and his wife, Nurse Ellie."

Doc James was a tall, handsome man and younger than she thought he'd be. His wife was quite pretty, her red dress and long dark hair held back in a neat chignon. The doc got out first, then went to his wife's side to help her out. She kissed his cheek in return and gave him a smile. He was looking at her as if her and Russell weren't present.

All of a sudden, Nurse Ellie turned and waved. "Hello. Where is the patient?"

"In here," Russell called out.

The two didn't waste any time, but hurried inside to Widow Young. They spent the latter part of an hour in the room with the door closed.

Russell paced back and forth on the porch while Naomi got him another cup of coffee. He looked down at the dark liquid with a frown. "What I need is a shot of whiskey!"

"A shot of whiskey won't help. It will make you numb and not feel anything." Naomi had seen many men lose their soul drinking whiskey, and other hardened liquor. It was the ruin of many men.

"Exactly. Maybe I'd rather feel nothing."

She placed a hand on her hip. "Russell Young, you surprise me wanting whiskey this time of morning!"

"I'm sorry, just nervous about Ma. What if she loses her leg or her ability to walk again? Then what? It will kill her, she is not the type of person to be home bound and helpless, depending on anyone."

Russell was scared. Like a small child, he didn't want to face his mother may be weakened. Naomi's heart went out to him. She laid a hand on his arm. "She'll be fine. Have some faith in her ability to heal."

"You're right. I'm jumping the gun, aren't I?" He leaned his forehead against hers. It made Naomi's heart skip a beat.

"Yes, Russell. Let's wait and see what the doctor says."

Wesley came outside so Naomi stepped back. "Are they still in with Ma?"

Wesley stuffed his hands in his pocket, rocking back on his heels and nodded his head. "They're taking an awful long time."

Naomi watched the two brothers exchange worst case scenarios. They truly worried about their Ma and she understood. They had a loving mother all their lives, one who never left their side, provided and protected them.

Her mother had given her up. Same with her father, whoever he was. She'd never known, didn't ever recall anyone being kind and loving. Sometimes, at night, she'd have visions of a small room cluttered with clothes and a mattress on the floor where she slept with another kid the same age as her. She had to be five, maybe six, it was hard to determine. A woman was always in the background but she wasn't sweet and kind. No. She was angry and sad, her dark blue eyes looking at Naomi as if she hated her.

For many years, Naomi tried to forget those mean eyes staring at her with so much hate. She often wondered what had happened to the other little girl she had shared a mattress with. The girl had blonde hair just like hers. Was she her sister? She didn't recall. All she remembered was the other girl was there one day and gone the next.

Then, the horrible woman with those ugly blue eyes disappeared, leaving her alone. Naomi had gone hungry for a long time, she remembered, and ventured outside looking for something to eat.

When she tried to get back inside, there were men there, sifting through the clothes and placing things in boxes. They shooed her away, told her the place was abandoned.

Naomi had nowhere to go. She remembered walking the streets and alleys, looking for the blonde woman with the hateful eyes. She searched for her day and night, asking everyone she came into contact with but no one saw her. Then, an older lady took her in, allowing Naomi to stay with her in a hidden place in an abandoned building. The woman taught her how to make it on the streets. She showed her how to beg for money, to steal and stash food to last for days on end.

With the old woman's help, she learned to live on the streets, dodging truant officers and taking care of herself when she realized she had been abandoned. Then Millie had died, and she was alone again.

When she watched Russell and Wesley together, their concern for their Ma glowing in their eyes, she wished she had that, too. All she had was a dream that had died a long time ago. She wasn't even sure what the dream was any more.

Now she had to give up any chance of having a normal life because she wasn't going to ruin someone else's life. She stared at Russell as he spoke with Wesley, his eyes lighting up when he spoke of his mother. He deserved a real woman, someone decent, without a horrible past. He needed someone he was able to trust.

It wasn't her. She had lied from the beginning. If he ever found out, he'd never trust her again. It was why she was going to leave here, to go before he found out what kind of horrible person she was.

Was it fair? Who knew!

It was breaking her heart.

Relief surged through Naomi when Doc James came outside to stand on the porch. He was smiling so that was a great sign.

"How is she, Doc?" Wesley and Russell asked at the exact same time.

He grinned. "She's fine, boys. A small strain but sometimes that can be worse. If she doesn't stay in bed for at least a week, it won't heal. She's not too happy about having to do so."

Naomi stepped up. "What can we do to help?"

He nodded to Naomi. "I suggest compresses three times a day to keep the swelling down. In about five days, she'll be able to get up more but the ankle will have to be wrapped for support. My wife can show you how to wrap it if you would like to go inside."

"I'll go right in," she told him, excusing herself. This meant she'd have to stay for another week at least. Secretly, she wanted to stay forever but if she had a week, then at least she'd be able to plan how to leave.

Naomi spent the morning learning how to apply cool compresses to Widow Young's ankle and to wrap the foot and ankle when the time came for her to get up.

She was not a happy patient and constantly complained. Naomi took it all in stride, warning the older woman if she didn't listen her foot would crack into pieces and fall off.

"Naomi, that's nonsense! Are you trying to scare me?"

"Yes, is it working?"

"No it isn't. I feel useless this way. I have to do something!"

"I'm going to need you to tell me how to feed your sons. Did Russell tell you about the disaster last night?"

"He mentioned that I may want to stick with you awhile until you learned a little more."

Her kind words made Naomi smile. "I think I need you terribly. I can't follow directions for the life of me."

"Okay, that makes me happy. If you give me a pencil and some paper, I'll make a list of ingredients for tonight's supper. Have you made breakfast yet for the boys?"

She shook her head. "No, Nora sent flapjacks and eggs for breakfast. Would you like to eat now that the doctor has gone?"

"I'm not too hungry but if you can butter a slice of bread along with a cup of coffee, that will suffice until later."

Naomi went to work in the kitchen, taking whipped butter and smearing it on a thick slice of fresh bread. After placing it on a plate, she poured fresh coffee and delivered the food. Widow Young didn't look up as she was so busy writing away.

"I'll be back to discuss supper in awhile," Naomi told her, exiting the room. She sat at the table, sipping coffee and picked up a flapjack. Nibbling on the end, she stared into space, wondering what it would be like if she didn't have to leave. Her mother-in-law was so kind, offering to teach her whatever she needed.

Russell was anxious to consummate the marriage, that much she knew. Except she wasn't going to let it go that far. She didn't dare. He deserved more.

Naomi stood, her mind made up. Perhaps it was time to make Russell dislike her. Then it wouldn't be so hard when she had to turn and walk away.

## Chapter 7

Ever since Naomi decided to stay at the farm house, he'd been lonely without her. Even though he'd stayed here by himself as a single man, it wasn't the same now that he'd married her. Wesley sat on the front porch of the cabin with him, listening to him complain.

"I have a bride and haven't been able to sleep in the same bed with her yet. What kind of marriage did I wind up with?"

Wesley laughed. "Brother, it's not like its everyday something like this happens to Ma. You know we can't take care of her all day long, we have work to do. Why don't you go visit her? Sit on the porch with her instead of out here whining with me?"

"I tried last night. She cut me off, said Ma needed her. Naomi shut the door so fast my head spun."

"Maybe you didn't approach things right. If it were my wife, I'd be showing her how romantic I can be. Why, it's not everyday a bride falls into a marriage like this and has to go off and care for her mother-in-law. It takes a special lady to do that and you haven't even thanked her yet."

"How in the world does a man do that?" Russell didn't have a clue. Why, he was lucky to have her, what else did she need to know?

Wesley shook his head. "You sure don't know squat about women. Your next move is to pour gifts unto her feet. Yes, with flowers and some of that special chocolate Jim Wheeler has shipped in at the mercantile in Wichita Falls."

"I was thinking more like spending time in the cow barn showing her how to milk Dolly. I can wrap my arms around her and feel her softness and steal a few kisses in between."

Wesley slapped him on the back. "Brother, you can do that too but buy her something nice. A city girl like her is probably used to lots of gifts."

Russell had to agree. He forgot she was a rich girl who was used to things. Why didn't she act like it then? He expected her to be a bit more snobbish and she was far from acting like an uppity city girl. "You know, you're probably right. I'll go first thing tomorrow and get her some presents."

After Wesley left, he spent the remainder of the evening watching the lights in the farmhouse until the last one was extinguished. His wife was still there, waiting on his Ma hand and foot. After four days, he was ready for her to come home. Wesley was there at night if his Ma needed anything. Why didn't she come home?

Was he too unsuited for her? He swore she enjoyed the kisses they shared by the way she curled into his arms and kissed him back. Then why did she behave all of a sudden as if his touch made her cringe?

Yesterday evening, he took hold of her hand and she pulled it away as if his touch scalded her skin. He was surprised when she closed the door in his face telling him she had to take care of his Ma.

Ever since then, he'd been second guessing himself, wondering what a beautiful, well-bred city girl would want with him. He began to be suspicious though. He may be a farm boy, but perhaps there was more to Naomi than meets the eye. What was she afraid of?

He was going to get to the bottom of things first thing in the morning.

<> <>

Dolly had been antsy this morning while Russell milked her. He wondered if a storm wasn't brewing. The sky was bright blue, with no sign of storm clouds and yet whenever she behaved skittish a storm was almost certain to come in the preceding days.

He was determined though to get to Wichita Falls first thing this morning so if a storm was in the works, it had better wait until he got back.

He went to the main farm house to check on Ma while Naomi busied herself in the kitchen, ignoring him except for an occasional nod his way. Flapjacks were setting on the table, steam wafting from the plate while Wesley sat down and helped himself.

Satisfied his Ma was doing well he sat at the table, waiting for Naomi to join them. When she didn't, he glared at her while filling his plate. She had to know he was not pleased. Her skittish attitude was beginning to anger him. She was his wife, why did he deserve to be treated with disdain? What had he done to her?

He wasn't able to keep quiet any longer. "Naomi, please join us."

She shook her head. "I'm sorry, I'm in the middle of putting together a pie. I have to cut up the peaches from the orchard outside and then work on the pie dough which has given me trouble lately. It's very hard to do. You go ahead, enjoy your breakfast."

Her rambling made him even more angry. What was her issue? He stared at his brother, who looked up and shrugged before shoveling more food into his mouth. Wesley finished up and left, mumbling about being behind schedule.

That left Russell and Naomi in the kitchen, alone. He was going to get to the bottom of things, right here, right now. "Naomi, we have to talk."

He watched her back as her hands stopped moving. She was peeling the peaches and her hands froze in mid-air, one hand holding a fruit, the other holding the knife. "What do you want to talk about? I'm very busy."

"Us." He slid the chair back, walking up behind her, placing his hands on her waist. He breathed in the rose scent she wore. Closing his eyes, he nuzzled the back of her neck.

She sucked in a deep breath. He heard it. That meant she was still interested in him, didn't it? It gave him hope. "I am going into town today. When I get back later, I want us to spend some time together, you and I."

"We can't. Your Ma."

He kissed her neck.

She shivered.

He smiled. "Ma can be alone for a little bit, even the doc said so. Besides, Wesley is here to keep an eye on her, too. You need to get away from all this and relax."

"I'm fine, really. No need to get away."

"It's not a request. It's an order. I'm your husband, I need you."

He left her there, staring after him. As he went out the door, he saw her look, those blue eyes following him as he closed the door.

It was time they consummated this marriage.

Tonight.

He wasn't going to take no for an answer. Not that he was going to force her, he didn't mean to put that in her head. He wanted to give her gifts, make her feel wanted and make this marriage real before the thirty days were up. He wasn't about to let her go. Not now, not in two weeks.

Not ever.

She was his and he wanted her to know how much she was loved.

Maybe he wasn't able to give her fancy gifts like the rich city men were able to but if she wanted that kind of life, she'd still be there in the city. She'd have married one of them rich boys but she hadn't. Instead, she was here, with him.

She chose him.

He was going to feed off of that and make her his.

Tonight and forever.

Satisfied, he saddled his mare and left for Wichita Falls. An hour later with his mind filled with thoughts of tonight, he rode up to the mercantile and went inside.

"Hello, Mr. Young. How is married life?"

The woman's voice startled him. It was the lady who ran the boarding house. She was placing her purchases on the counter while Jim Wheeler added everything up.

"Married life is eluding me, Miss Addie." He wondered if she'd care to speak with him about his bride. After all, she was the matchmaker. Maybe she'd be able to help. "Do you have a moment?"

"Certainly." She spoke to Mr. Wheeler and excused herself. Taking his arm, they walked to a far corner of the store to a quiet place. "Now, what can I do for you?"

"I was wondering if you would know what kind of gift to buy my wife? I think she's used to those fancy rich men. I'm actually starting to think she isn't interested in being married to a farmer."

Miss Addie's face fell. "Oh, dear! Mr. Young, I will be home in approximately one half hour. If you don't mind, stop by and we'll have some tea. I think there are some things we need to discuss in private."

Tea wasn't his favorite drink but he was curious why she wanted to talk and not answer his question right now. He nodded and arranged to meet her as she gathered her purchases and left. Russell spent a few minutes looking around before he found the chocolates, choosing a box that was supposed to come from a place called Belgium. He figured she'd like that, it sounded fancy.

Russell stopped by Jenna's café for some pastries to surprise his wife. The owner, after finding out he wanted them to surprise his wife, wrapped the pastries in brown paper and tied with a pretty string. He placed them in his saddle bag and rode up the street to the boarding house. It was time to find out what Miss Addie knew.

Word was she was the best matchmaker this side of the Mississippi. Miss Addie had a reputation for finding the men in the area good, Christian wives. It was one of the reasons his Ma and Nora arranged a bride through her.

He knocked on the front door to have it opened immediately. "Come in," Miss Addie acknowledged. "Right this way."

When they were seated at her table, he felt quite out of place. A white fancy tablecloth covered the wood table, along with a silver tray and little porcelain tea cups. She sent one his way. He looked down. How in the world was he going to pick up that tiny cup?

As he looked up, he watched Miss Addie grab the cup instead of the tiny handle and lift it to her mouth. She raised a brow to let him know he was to do the same. What if he spit out the awful tasting tea? He hated tea. Maybe if he pretended to drink the tea she wouldn't notice.

She placed the cup back on the table before he got a chance to drink any. She gave a heavy sigh. "Mr. Young, I'm afraid we have an issue that I feel must be taken care of. Please tell me why your bride is not being kind to you?"

"Naomi was fine a few days ago. I thought we were getting along great. We even, you know, were about to consummate the marriage if you know what I mean."

"Yes, I do. Go on."

"Then a bison almost broke into our cabin and we had to shoot him dead. After that, my Ma twisted her ankle and needed someone to care for her. Instead of allowing my brother Wesley, who lives in the house with Ma, Naomi insisted on staying there and has left me alone all week. She refuses to come home at night. Every chance I get she avoids me. She won't look me in the eye. There is something wrong and I can't put my finger on it. I'm losing her before I even had a chance to make this marriage work."

He'd never given anyone so much information before. Why did this woman bring out the need for him to spill the beans about his relationship with Naomi?

Miss Addie reached across the table and patted his hand. "I want you to listen carefully. In most cases, I never interfere in a relationship. However, this is not a normal situation."

"What do you mean, it isn't normal?"

"I must be getting soft in my old age. I usually leave it up to the other party when there is something that needs taken care of. Here's the issue, Mr. Young. I was waiting for Naomi to talk to you about this but

I believe she is truly afraid to. I'm also worried if you don't take action immediately, she may not stick around after the thirty days are up. You will need to do something now, for her sake as well as your own."

"What did I do?" He was stumped! "I gave her plenty of room to get used to living on a farm. I realize she is from the city but if she wanted a rich man, she'd have gotten one by now. No man can resist her, she's beautiful."

"It's not that, Mr. Young. Naomi hasn't been totally honest with you. She's ashamed more so than anything and I asked her to tell you after I found out the truth. It was easy to spot."

He stared at Miss Addie. His bride lied to him? "What hasn't she told me the truth about?"

"I wish I didn't have to do this, it is totally against my grain. However, you are the kind of man that would not hold this against someone."

His brow rose. Miss Addie was not the type of woman to falter. He was right. "Go on," he told her, curious as to why his bride lied and this woman felt the need to butt in and tell him the truth.

"The truth of the matter is Naomi is not from a well-bred family. She is an orphan. She lied because she didn't think you would want her if you knew where she came from."

Russell stared at the older woman. He didn't know what to say. A sense of relief actually washed over him knowing she wasn't some uppity city girl. He shook his head. "Now I understand more than ever. The signs were all there." He even laughed. "Did you know she tried so hard to act like she was this fancy lady and almost broke her neck in the process."

"Thank goodness she didn't break her neck! I see you are not angry. Although, she promised she would tell you."

"I think she tried to tell me the night the bison came into our yard." He was almost sure before that hairy monster interfered. Russell grinned at the way Naomi had described the bison. After that, his Ma got hurt and for some reason she was bent on avoiding him.

"Then I'm sure she has plans to tell you. Although I'm not sorry to have told you first, it is imperative you secure your marriage within the next week."

"I'm not so convinced she will. For some reason, she is avoiding me. What if she decides she doesn't want to stay here and when the thirty days are up, she leaves."

Miss Addie patted him on the top of his hand. "Oh, son, I'm afraid you may be missing the point. Naomi is an orphan. She has nowhere to go. If she does decide she isn't good enough for you, she'll leave here. But, there will be no destination for her in mind. We promised a return ticket. She'd have to go back to the city, with no home to go to."

"You think that's what she'd do, sacrifice a good home for the streets? Why?"

Miss Addie shook her head. "An orphan has nothing. Many have come through my matchmaking agency thinking they were not worthy of a new life. Maybe it's time to speak with your wife before the time is up."

He nodded. "I will, I promise. Now that I understand her reasoning, it makes sense. Thank you, Miss Addie, I'll consider everything you said."

"Good. Then I hope I don't see her a week from Saturday." She stood, walking him to the door. "Just remember, if you are too aggressive, it may cause her to be scared and run off."

"I bought her gifts."

"That will be nice, but I doubt gifts will solve the problem. Make sure you let her know you can't live without her. She's worthy to be your wife will be the most important thing you can tell her."

Russell's mare was a little skittish. He gazed up at the sky, noticing the storm clouds rolling in. Sometimes, a quick storm was right on the horizon, ready to pound the earth and then before anyone knew what was happening, it was over.

This didn't look like that type of storm. Thunder clapped in the background. It sounded far away but Russell knew better. He had an hour to get back and hoped that was enough time, else he'd be stuck along the road somewhere.

"You may want to stay until the storm runs its course," Miss Addie pointed out.

He had thought of it but wanted to get back to Naomi. Besides, he had fresh pastries for her. "I'll take my chances. Good-day." Russell rode out of town a little faster than he normally did.

Passing the waterfalls, he noticed the sky getting black. That didn't give him much time. "Go on, get moving," he told his mare as if she understood his commands.

He was ten minutes from home, relief flooding over him the rain hadn't started yet. Russell didn't mind rain so much but thunder and lightening flashed in the distant sky. If it came any closer, he'd have to take cover for awhile. Hopefully, he'd make it home before that.

Except all of a sudden it came at a speed Russell wasn't counting on. He was usually good at deciphering when a storm would hit, but today he had his mind on getting back to Naomi. It probably altered his thinking.

The rain came so fast there was no time to throw on the coat in his saddlebag. Water dumped down over the trail, washing away stone and dirt, making it hard for his mare to keep going. When a bolt of lightening flashed too close for comfort, his mare stumbled. He knew it was time to take shelter. She was one of the newer horses, he had trained her but she wasn't as familiar to storms like this as the others.

Russell left the trail when he noticed a large oak tree with decent cover. He slid from his mare and guided her to a dry spot underneath the branches. They stood there for awhile, watching the torrents of rain pelt the earth. It had been quite awhile since they had a storm of this nature in the area. God knew they needed some good rains.

Except he was in a hurry to get home and talk to Naomi. He didn't want to waste one more minute without telling his bride how he felt. He could understand her hesitation since she had lied to him, but he didn't even care about this particular lie. It was a lie to protect herself from all she'd been through. If he had been in her shoes, perhaps he'd have done the same thing.

If he didn't have his family to see him through, Russell didn't know how he'd react. Even when they found out their father was none other than Nora White's husband and they had three half-brothers, at least he had his family members to rely on to get him through. Naomi had no one. Absolutely no one.

He wasn't about to let her leave.

Not now.

Not ever.

She was his and he was going to get home and tell her! Not even a storm of this nature will stop him!

# Chapter 8

What a darn fool he was! Russell groaned. The mare was long gone by now. Here he was, stuck with his leg caught under a heavy branch. If she hadn't been spooked, he'd have been able to reach the rope hanging from the end of the saddle and tie it to the branch. If she were his trained mare, he'd have been able to instruct her how to pull it off his leg.

But no, he was stupid to take a new horse out for the first time knowing a thunderstorm was brewing. It wasn't her fault. Russell prayed she'd go back to the farm a few miles away and not wander off somewhere. Otherwise, he'd have to spend days, maybe longer, looking for her. After he got the heavy limb off his leg, of course.

He sighed. Lying on his back, he twisted his head, trying to peek through the leaves to see rain still coming down. The limb that fell was so large, the leaves so thick it almost buried him. This was one storm he hadn't counted on. Storms around here would come and go, most finished in a short time. Not today. It was well over thirty minutes since the rain started.

Earlier, he had decided not to wait out the storm. He just got up in the saddle when a horrendous crack followed by lightening frightened the mare. She had reared up and he tried to hang on but when a branch cracked him on the back, it took him off guard. He fell to the ground just as another larger branch came down hard to trap his lower leg.

The mare reared again, turning and galloping off in the storm. He had called for her, to no avail. At least she was heading in the right direction, he hoped. It was still early enough someone may come by. They'd be crazy to be out in this storm though.

Russell tried to sit up but each time he did, the back of his neck and head began to ache so bad he got dizzy and was unable to focus. The way the smaller branch hit him probably gave him a concussion. When he felt his head, there was a lump the size of an egg on his skull.

If he didn't return home by nightfall, he knew Wesley would begin to look for him. Maybe if he laid here for awhile, the head would stop hurting and he'd be able to get this limb off his trapped leg. The limb was heavy but nothing he couldn't pry off himself if his head didn't stop spinning.

He'd give it a few minutes. Perhaps take a little nap. Yes, that's what he'd do.

<> <>

Nightfall was just over the horizon. In another hour, the farm and surrounding area would be cloaked in darkness. Wesley had carried his Ma out to the table to eat supper. "I am allowed to walk with a cane, son. Doc James said I can put a little pressure on my foot. You don't need to baby me." She looked around. "I thought Russell would be back by now," she said to them, a crease at her brow. "He usually isn't gone this long."

Naomi was starting to worry, too. "He did say when he returned today from Wichita Falls, we were going to spend some time together."

Wesley raised a brow, even stopped eating. "That a fact? He probably got caught in the thunderstorm and is waiting it out."

Naomi looked outside. "The storms been over for some time now."

Wesley slid his chair back. "I'm going to saddle up one of the mares and go down the road a bit."

Naomi knew Wesley was worried by the way his face looked so serious. He was usually calm by nature, but he had an anxious expression right now. If he was concerned, there may be cause to worry.

Taking a deep breath, she nodded when he left, chancing a look at Widow Young.

The Widow set her fork down. She clasped her hands together. "Something is wrong. I feel it with every breath I take."

Naomi went to her, giving her a hug. "Now, now. Russell is fine."

The moment she said the words, the screen door burst open. Wesley's eyes were huge!

"What is it?" Naomi asked, her heart in her throat.

"Russell's mare was at the barn, still saddled up. I went through the whole building looking for Russell but he's not there. There is no way my brother would leave a horse outside in this kind of weather. This mare is pretty new to us. I think she got spooked and he's out there somewhere."

"Oh, my, no!" Widow Young began to cry. "I knew something wasn't right."

Naomi had to be strong. The thought of losing Russell was never a consideration. She tried to squelch down the fear that began to rise inside of her. She didn't want to panic!

"I'm going to get Rusty and a few of the hands from next door, see if we can scout the area before it gets too dark. Keep Ma calm, Naomi."

Naomi had her arms around Widow Young. She nodded to Wesley, almost in tears herself.

He looked in to her eyes. "I will find my brother," he promised.

"I know you will."

She was beginning to understand the bond between siblings. Even though she never had any, what she witnessed in the last few weeks being here was something she had always longed for. She just hoped it wasn't too late for the two of them. *Dear Lord, surround Russell with angels no matter where he is and keep him safe until we find him. Amen.*

For the next hour, Naomi paced back and forth in between checking on Widow Young. She had settled the older woman onto the settee by the window so his Ma was able to keep an eye on the horizon. Naomi thought it would keep her calm if she was actively looking for her son this way.

Naomi stopped pacing to listen when Widow Young began to speak. "My late husband got caught in a lightening storm. We had been here about two years, the house was built and the barn just got finished when his horse threw him. I waited all night long for him to come home. Sitting here, by the window, waiting, watching. I sat on a wooden chair he had made with his own hands. When daylight came, I knew he wasn't coming back."

Naomi gasped. "Maybe it's not a good idea to sit by the window. I'm sure Russell is fine."

"I don't know if my heart can stand another break."

Naomi wrapped her arms around her. The woman was falling apart. "Be strong, Widow Young, please. He'll be okay, I know he will."

She patted Naomi's hand. "I'm sure he'll be fine." A sob caught at her throat. "It's because of you I'm falling apart. If you weren't here, I would try to be stronger. With you here, I can let my emotions out because I know you will comfort me. Thank you, Naomi, you are a blessing."

No one had ever told her she was a blessing. All her young life she had been called an ungrateful urchin. When Widow Young looked her in the eye with gratitude, Naomi knew she was telling the truth. This past week the two had gotten real close.

Naomi pulled a wooden chair away from the table and set it alongside her. She sat down and faced Russell's mother. It was time to be honest. Maybe now was not the time but it certainly would take Widow Youngs mind off of her son, at least for a few minutes.

Fearful of being rejected, she almost didn't blurt it out until Widow Young gave her a curious look. "What is it, Naomi? What's wrong?"

Naomi clasped her hands together on her lap. "I haven't been honest with Russell or Wesley or you." She had vowed to keep quiet before it was no longer an option. Naomi had some morals left.

Widow Young shook her head. "What do you mean?"

It was hard to be honest. She had lived most of her life hiding in alleys, stealing for food and waiting for hand outs until she went to the orphanage. If Widow Young rejects her, then her sons will, also. Naomi was afraid she'd die if she had to go back to that life. She wanted to stay here. It was beginning to feel like home. Even an orphan knew right from wrong. She'd never be able to live with herself if she didn't speak up.

"Go on, spit it out. It's not going to come out on its own."

Naomi hung her head, unable to look her in the eye. "I lied. When I sent the letter to Miss Addie, I made everything up. I am not from a well to do family. I didn't live in a fancy house on 5th Avenue. It's all lies."

Widow Young grinned. She took Naomi's hands in her own. "Look at me, dear."

Naomi slowly raised her head to look at her mother-in-law. There was no rage, no anger there. "I'm sorry."

"No need to be. I was waiting for you to come out with the truth. From our very first conversation, I had a feeling you weren't from upper crust. Do you know how I know this?"

Naomi was too upset to speak. She shook her head.

"I was upper crust, my dear. Before my late husband swept me off my feet, my family had a house in San Francisco most people long for. I grew up there, never wanting for anything. Then a handsome miner caught my eye, with promises to take me to Texas and build me the biggest ranch I'd ever seen. He was going to hit pay-dirt, he had said. He didn't. He made enough to buy us this farm and we were truly happy until the night he never came back."

"I'm sorry. It must've been hard for you with two children."

Widow Young gave her a smile. "I'm afraid I have secrets of my own, Naomi. My boys are not from my husband. Since you will be here a long time, you should know, and maybe you already do. Their father is the deceased husband of Nora Young."

"What!" Naomi's eyes widened. She didn't know what to say so she said nothing. Her mouth tried to ask another question but failed.

"It's true, sadly. I wish with all my heart those boys were my late husbands. Please don't judge me. I didn't ask for Mr. White's advances. He took advantage of me while I was in a vulnerable state, I realize this now."

"I'm so sorry. Does Russell know?"

"Yes, he always knew. I never tried to hide it from him. Although we did hide it from Nora for ten long years. When she found out it was not very nice around here but we all worked it out. We're all friends now. So, don't you see, Naomi, you can work this out, too. I love you like a daughter."

"Thank you." Naomi was almost in tears. She never thought she'd be accepted for being an urchin. "I'm afraid I know nothing about being a housewife."

A smile spread across the widow's cheek. "That, my dear, will be my job to show you. Oh, look!" She pointed out the window.

A distant glare from torches lit up a line of riders coming in. Naomi flew out the door, standing on the porch, leaning hard over the bannister. "They're coming this way!" Her heart beat against her chest so hard and fast she took in a deep breath of fresh night air to slow it down.

Was it him? Was he hurt? When she noticed Widow Young behind her, she helped the woman to the rocker on the porch. "Please, sit. You can see from here."

The riders made their way down the path that led to the farm. Instead of bringing him to the farmhouse, they turned towards the cabin. Naomi ran towards the riders, holding up her skirts and going as fast as she was able.

She got to the porch in time to open the front door as they hoisted an unconscious Russell and brought him inside. They placed him on the bed. Immediately, Naomi got busy pulling off his wet, mud soaked boots. She looked up to see a group of men standing in the doorway.

"Wesley, go let your Ma know he's alright before she tries to walk down here on her own."

He hurried out. The others tipped their hat. Rusty, the smaller, older man with a head full of red hair offered assistance. "I'll be heading to get the doc as soon as daylight breaks. No sense in going out in the night. He hit his head pretty hard. Looks like his foot is swollen but not broken. Darn lucky that tree didn't break a bone."

"What happened?" Naomi poured water from the basin into the bowl, swishing a rag around and twisting it as water fell back into the bowl.

"Looks like lightening hit a tree branch and spooked the horse. The limb fell on Russell's leg but it wasn't too heavy for him to remove. Looks like his head injury is what kept him down. We're gonna have to get the doc here to take a look. I think the leg is fine."

"Much obliged for your help. All of you." Naomi's confidence was returning to her. Now that she knew Widow Young didn't care if she was a fraud, she prayed others would feel the same way. Hopefully, she didn't need to tell anyone and she'd be able to put it all behind her.

Except for one man. Her husband. She had to tell him sooner or later. Right now, his health was all that matters. His face looked so white as if all the blood had drained from their vessels. His clothes were soaked, pasted against his skin. "I'm going to need to get him into warm, clean clothes. Can one or two of you help?"

Twenty minutes later Russell was propped up on the bed with fresh, clean clothes and a blanket covering him to his neck. It looked as if the blood was returning to his skin. She kept wringing out a damp cloth and applying it to his forehead, sitting on the edge of the bed while patting it over his skin. He winced a few times but stayed asleep.

The lump on his head wasn't getting any larger so that was a good sign. She knew, even though she wasn't trained as a nurse that a knot on the head that is growing is a bad sign.

Wesley tapped on the door. "I hope you don't mind, I let myself in."

"It's fine. How's your mother?"

"She's settled in for the night. I assured her he was fine and you were taking care of Russell. She wanted to come down here herself but when I told her that he already has a wife to take care of him, she agreed."

"Thank you. She needs to take care of herself. I'm sure he'll be up and about in no time."

Three days later, Russell was still unconscious. Naomi was getting worried. The doc handed her a bottle of laudanum, instructing her to keep him as still as possible. She had to force the liquid down his throat several times a day.

Widow Young had settled herself in the chair by his bed, insisting on sitting with him while Naomi got some rest. "You must be strong for him. Now go and take in some fresh air."

She was right. Naomi hadn't left his side in three days. She caught site of herself in the mirror by the door. Was that the same woman who came here a few weeks ago? Blue eyes were puffy and tired, her hair was in a messy bun. She didn't much care, her job was to make sure Russell woke up.

The doctor had reduced his medicine yesterday, telling her to give less each day, that he will slowly wake. He did look worried though. If a doctor looked worried, should she be?

When she confronted the doc he said to have faith. Most people recovered from head injuries and they were tricky. It was why he had given the medicine to keep him still and sleeping but now it was time for him to wake, if he wakes up.

If he didn't, then what?

No, she had to have faith.

There was no way she wanted to live here on the farm without him.

Not now.

Not ever.

Widow Young was right. She had to get some air. Naomi made her way to the barn to find Wesley sitting on a stool milking Dolly. Her tail swiped him in the head several times when he forgot to duck. It was almost comical.

When she laughed out loud, Wesley turned his head. He smiled. "Dolly doesn't like anyone except Russell milking her."

"I noticed." She wrapped her arms around her, slowly making her way closer. When Dolly saw her, she lifted her head.

"He was looking forward to showing you how to milk Dolly, you know."

"He was?"

"Yes, he told me so."

"We have to have faith, Wesley." She heard the defeat in his voice. "He will wake up."

Wesley turned to her, a haunted look in his eyes. "This is the worst thing ever. I keep walking in circles trying to will him to wake up. He's on my mind every single waking moment. I love my brother with all my heart."

"I love him, too. He knows he is loved. Let's give him a fighting chance."

A deep sigh escaped Wesley. "I'll try. He looks so, so, awful. His skin is pale and drawn and I can't see any life in him. I am so worried."

"Worry gets you nowhere, so you best do your chores and carry on. He is counting on you." Where did that come from? She wasn't good at taking over, ordering others around. Or, was she? Actually, Naomi had no clue what she was capable of, she was never given the chance.

Except for now. Right now, right here, this moment. Her job was to keep things running smoothly, to reassure everyone her husband was going to survive his fall and come out of this fighting. There was no other way to think or feel.

*Russell Young! You get up and show the world you are still alive and well, right this minute!*

## Chapter 9

Russell stirred. He felt a warm hand in his but wasn't able to open his eyes, although he tried. "Naomi?" Was she here? He wanted to see her but his lids were so heavy. Darkness surrounded him. If only he was able to see her.

"It's Ma." He heard the tears in her voice. His Ma was here. Good. She was always here for him. For Wesley, too. The three were always here for each other, the bond was so strong.

"I can't open my eyes." It was hard to speak, his words came out raspy, hurting his throat.

"Don't try. Go to sleep. You need to rest. The doc said you will wake up slowly. Sleep now, son. It's alright."

He knew she was right. His Ma never lied to him. Where was Naomi? Shouldn't she be here, too, wherever here was. He wasn't sure if he was in his own bed or at Ma's house. It didn't matter, he was so tired, his body drained of all strength, his emotions, they were jumbled up in his head.

A soft hand took his free one. "Naomi," he whispered and smiled. It was her. He knew it without seeing her.

"I'm here. Hush, your Ma is right. Sleep now."

"Kiss me first."

"Russell, I, you should sleep."

"I can't," he mumbled. "Not until you kiss me."

<><>

She leaned forward and placed a kiss on his cheek but he turned his head and their lips met. Naomi closed her eyes, grateful he was starting to come out of his stupor. It was a sign that all was well in the world. God was answering prayers.

Finally.

Not that she wasn't grateful or demanding God to hurry, but it had been a few awfully long, heart wrenching days.

Relief washed over her like water that fell from the waterfall near Wichita Falls.

His breathing became steady as his chest moved up and down, the cords at his neck relaxing. He still held her hand as if letting go was the last thing he wanted to do. The kiss seemed to settle him down. Naomi looked at his Ma and shrugged.

"I need to get supper started," Naomi told her.

"I'll stay with him. It's fine. Go."

"Thank you, Widow Young."

"Please, call me Catherine."

Naomi was honored to be allowed to call his mother by her first name. She kept a smile on her face while cooking a supper of chicken pieces and broth, along with some rice and a few vegetables. Catherine may have been out of commission due to her sprained ankle but she had instructed Naomi well on several dishes.

Naomi felt comfortable cooking now. She wasn't all thumbs when it came to measuring everything. Yesterday, she had spent time labeling the flour, sugar and salt so there would be no more mistakes.

She stood back while the kettle boiled. Her bread was in the oven browning, her lemonade sitting in the pitcher on the table and the chicken soup was almost done. If only Russell was awake enough to really enjoy her first successful meal. Even so, he needed to eat, so she'd have to spoon feed him.

Catherine was walking with a cane, although it was slow progress. She did well on her own, so there was no use trying to tell her to stay put. As Naomi finished supper, his mother kept her company, telling stories of the two brothers when they were younger.

"I had to constantly fetch them from the barn to come in for supper. They'd play soldier and cowboys and Indians, jumping from the loft area."

Naomi laughed. "Sounds like they were active children. I watched kids playing on swings and slides in the park but had to sneak in after dark in order to play. Usually, it was by myself, unless there were other orphans nearby."

Catherine looked concerned. "You've had quite a rough life, haven't you?"

Naomi nodded. "I have but I'm not going to let that control my world any longer. I love this place. When Russell is back to normal, I'm going to spill the beans. Tell him the whole truth and let him decide if I am worthy to be his wife."

"Oh, honey, you are worthy. If you care for my son, and I have two good eyes that can clearly see you do then there is no need to worry. You don't have to be in a hurry to tell him, you know."

"Yes. I do. In another week our thirty days are up. I have to be honest with him now. I won't stay if he doesn't want me to."

"That's noble and all but are you sure it's the right thing to do? I know he won't care. Russell is a man of integrity. He will honor the marriage and I do believe he cares for you so very much. I can see it in the way he looks at you."

Naomi gave her a heartfelt smile. She closed her eyes and took in a deep breath. "Keeping this secret will bother me forever. All my life I've had to hide in places, steal food if I couldn't find a place to eat and my belly grumbled so badly. Hating and crying out to God for the fact I had to live that way. Feeling unwanted and unloved made me do what I did, pretending to be someone I wasn't. It's time it ends, even if I wind up losing everything."

Catherine hobbled to the stove, taking Naomi in her arms. "You won't lose everything. I admire your spirit and wanting to be honest and my son will, too. Do what's right in your heart."

"Thank you for understanding." Naomi was scared. She didn't want Catherine to know. What if Russell rejected her? It would be so easy to continue her lie, pretend she was from a wealthy family and try to make the best of things. Except her life had never been easy. So why start now?

"I'm going to sit and rest for awhile on the porch," Catherine told her. "Take a bowl of soup to Russell. I'm sure if you spoon feed him some nutrition he will awaken much faster."

"I've already done so." Naomi had ladled out a bowl to cool off some time ago. As Catherine made her way to the porch, Naomi gathered the bowl of soup, along with a spoon and glass of water.

She set everything on the table beside the bed, placing herself on the edge of the mattress to feed him easily. Taking his shoulder, she shook it gently as she didn't want to scare him. He began to stir. "Russell, it's Naomi. I brought you something to eat."

"I'm not hungry."

"You have to eat something."

"I'm hungry for another kiss."

She smiled. "If I give you a kiss will you take a spoonful of the soup?"

"Who made it?" She almost laughed out loud at his question. She didn't want to lie to him any more but if she told him it was from her, he'd probably refuse. Especially after the meals she had been making. "Who do you think?"

"Hmm, my Ma?"

"Here, take a spoonful." She tried to avoid answering him. He wasn't deterred.

"Kiss first."

This time Naomi did laugh out loud. She leaned over and gave him a kiss on his lips thinking to brush them lightly and he'd be satisfied. Instead, he picked up an arm and threw it over her shoulder, pulling her closer. Deepening the kiss, she was sure her soup would be cold by the time he finished.

She sat back and stared at him, his eyes wide open now. A smile crept on his face. Her heart elated seeing him so awake. "That was quite the kiss."

"Now I'm ready for the soup," he told her, still grinning like a man who had the world handed to him. "Unless you want to give me another kiss. Or, a kiss for each spoonful I eat. How about it?"

Naomi giggled. "Nonsense, sir. I doubt I can withstand so many kisses."

She took a spoonful and shoved it in his mouth before he said another word. His brow went up. "This is so good. I'm so hungry."

"Then eat, Russell. Kisses won't fill your belly and make you stronger."

He grinned at her words as she continued to feed him until Catherine hobbled in. "I thought I heard voices. How are you feeling, son?"

"I'm better. This soup is delicious, Ma."

Catherine sat on the chair she had placed beside the bed. "You can thank Naomi. She made the soup."

Another brow went up. "Impressive!"

Naomi blushed. It was the first compliment she had ever received. Her face heated up. "Oh! I forgot about the bread. I'll be right back."

She placed the soup bowl on the table and ran into the kitchen area. Catherine had already taken the bread from the heat to Naomi's delight. She sliced a nice chunk and slathered whipped butter on top. Turning to go back in the bedroom, she stopped dead in the doorway when she saw Russell sitting up chatting away while eating from his bowl of soup.

She placed her hands on her hips. "Russell Young! You tricked me into thinking you needed help eating. Look at you, feeding yourself!"

He grinned. "I kind of liked you feeding me," he told her. Naomi looked at Catherine's reaction.

His mother rolled her eyes and stood up, leaning heavily on the cane. "It's time I got back to my own house. Goodnight, dear." She gave Russell a kiss on his forehead.

"I'll walk you back, Catherine. It seems Russell is fine to eat his food by himself."

"Thank you, dear. That will be nice."

The two enjoyed a long stroll across the yard. By the time they got to Catherine's house, she was leaning heavily on Naomi's arm. It had been a lot for her to be on her feet so much. "I hope you go inside and try to rest. I promise I'll be over first thing in the morning to help with breakfast. Now that Russell is awake, he'll be up and about in no time."

"With your tender care, I have no doubt. Just don't baby him too much. You see what he is capable of."

Coming back across the yard, Naomi had to smile at what Catherine said. Russell was being tricky, pretending he wasn't able to eat. She had to keep her eyes and ears open when it came to him. Oh, she dreaded the talk they needed to have soon. Mentally, she had prepared herself for it but tonight, she just wanted a night of bliss.

Tomorrow.

She'd talk to him then.

Naomi almost stumbled on the first step when she reached the porch. "Careful, there."

Naomi screamed bloody murder and froze.

"It's me, Russell."

Her hand clutched at her throat. "Oh, my lands, Russell. You are supposed to be in bed."

"I'm fine. I've been in bed for too long. Look, my head is all healed." He went to stand up but wobbled to one side.

"My foot it is! Russell Young, take my arm and get back to bed immediately!"

He took her arm but stood there, refusing to move. "Only if you are there with me."

A flush began up one side of her face to the other. "Russell!"

"I insist. I won't be able to sleep without you there to keep me safe."

"That's ludicrous. I've slept fine on the settee." Even though it gave her tremendous back ache some nights.

"You are my wife, I could insist."

She tapped her foot. "Are you saying you would force me to lie with you."

He nodded. "Yes." Then he threw back his head and laughed. Then he yowled when she poked him in the ribs. "Ow, that hurts."

"Oh, Russell. Let's get you inside."

She took a step forward. He simply refused to move until she agreed.

After some time, Naomi did. "On one condition."

"What?"

"You allow me to take a buggy to Wichita Falls soon. The gown I wore coming here I want to sell and buy some material to learn to sew. The gown is way too fancy for a farmer's wife."

Russell tilted his head to one side. "I'll take you myself in a few days when the doc clears me. How does that sound?"

"Deal."

"One more condition," he told her.

Oh, boy, had she created a monster? "What?"

"We seal it with a kiss."

"If that is what it will take for me to get my way, then it's a deal."

He whipped his arm around her, pulling her close and placing a heart-stopping kiss that'd keep her up all night. Long after they had gone to bed, she was staring at the dark sky through the window in the bedroom, wondering what it would be like to truly become his wife in all ways.

If only she didn't have to tell him about her past.

Her heart was torn but she knew the right thing to do.

Tomorrow. She'd tell him tomorrow.

<> <>

Two days went by and they never had a chance to talk. Russell was up and about all day waiting for the doctor to show up. Doc gave him a clean slate, but made Russell promise not to do a whole lot of physical work for another week. Doc James cleared him for travel so she was excited they would be allowed to go to Wichita Falls soon.

He went to visit Dolly the minute the doc left. Naomi tip-toed outside to the barn, listening by the door, peeking in now and again to make sure he was not getting overwhelmed or overworking himself.

She didn't have to worry. That cow stood there and let him milk away, her tail missing his face as if she knew it was him. Naomi had witnessed the tail slapping Wesley in the face several times. A giggle erupted from her. Before she had a chance to slap a hand over her mouth Russell turned and smiled.

"Want to learn how to milk a cow?"

She made her way inside. "Sure."

Russell stood and offered her the bucket to sit on. She had to hike up her skirts, her knees apart, pushing all the material in between. As he instructed, she pulled on the teat, except the cow was being stubborn.

"Are you the only one she allows to milk her?"

"Do this," he insisted, placing an arm around her, leaning close and placing a hand over hers on the cows teat. He showed her how to move her hand, over and over until she finally got it to work.

Naomi shouted out. "It's so easy!"

Russell kissed her on the ear. "Go on, milk away."

They spent the remainder of the hour in the barn until Dolly got tired of them and began to get restless.

"Go on, Dolly. Get out of here!" Russell whistled to her.

Naomi laughed when she listened, heading out of the barn in easy strides. "This was fun. Thank you."

"I'm glad you came out to spy on me."

Naomi blushed. She hadn't wanted him to know how worried she was that he'd have a relapse. They were alone in the barn. Now was a good time to tell him about her past.

"I think we need to talk."

"Russell! Naomi!"

Wesley's voice carried in to the barn, meaning he was almost there.

"We'll talk later. Or do you want me to get rid of Wesley?"

"No, we can talk after supper."

He gave her a kiss on the forehead. She liked the attentive way he paid attention to her.

*Dear God, please let him understand. I don't want to give this up. I don't want to give him up.*

Wesley wanted Russell to go along to the White Ranch to look at a couple of new horses one of their half-brothers bought. "Adam got some fine horses at auction. He said to come on up and take a look."

Russell looked interested and waved to her as Wesley drove the buggy across their land towards the neighbors. The fence that had separated the two properties was still there except for a large area that had been cut out and a gate installed. Here of late the gate was left wide open for easy access back and forth. Maybe the kept it open because of all the things that kept happening.

Naomi waved to Catherine who was sitting on the front porch. "I'll be over in fifteen minutes," she shouted out.

Catherine waved. "No hurry, take your time."

Naomi hurried home to gather the fancy dress she wore the first day she had arrived. She had washed it and now hurried across the yard to use Catherine's ironing press to get all the wrinkles out.

"I have it heating on the stove, dear."

"Do you think I'll get enough for this to get enough material?"

"Yes, some ladies in town will kill for a dress of that nature. You'd be surprised what people buy. Have you and Russell talked about things yet?"

Naomi shook her head, concentrating on the material. "I'm afraid not. We haven't had a chance. I told him tonight after supper we need to talk."

"It's for the best, especially if you insist on doing so."

"I do. I want a clean slate no matter what the consequences." Although, she hoped somewhere deep down in her heart he'd understand and not send her away.

Naomi got a lesson in ironing while Catherine showed her how to carefully iron all the material to take the wrinkles out. They spent most of the morning at the table working away.

Naomi was trying so hard to be gentle and work the material like Catherine showed her she never heard Russell and Wesley enter the room until she felt his warm breath at her ear.

She jumped.

The iron almost dropped from her hand.

"Russell, you frightened me!"

"I'm sorry. Let me give you a kiss."

She leaned back and whispered. "Not in the presence of your Ma and brother."

He backed off, grinning.

Why was he being such a naughty devil? He'd come up behind her and try to steal kisses all the time. Was that how couples behaved? If so, she wanted him to keep doing this, except she didn't want to get her hopes up. She had to speak with him tonight, after supper. Nothing was going to stop her this time.

They ate supper at Catherine's house and stayed later than they had planned listening to Wesley's stories of how he had to take care of the farm while Russell lazed away in bed. Some of his facial expressions had everyone laughing. By the time they left, Naomi was yawning.

The walk across the yard was nice. Several times Russell pointed to a star cluster in the sky and when she'd look up, he'd wait until she looked over at him and steal a kiss. It took them a lot longer to get home. By the time they were on the porch, she insisted he sit on the porch. "I'll get us some lemonade. You sit and relax."

"I've been relaxing all night. Can I help?"

"No, sit."

Ten minutes later she had two glasses of fresh lemonade in her hands. It was too late, Russell was on the rocker, his head back, fast asleep.

Naomi stood there, holding the glasses, watching him. He was so handsome. She sighed, knowing another day had gone by and she wasn't able to tell him. Turning, she looked up into the sky, staring hard at the millions of tiny stars. "Maybe I should keep it to myself. Maybe my past isn't meant to be shared."

Setting the glasses down, Naomi stirred Russell, helping him inside. He was barely aware. He had to be exhausted and never complained or said a word to anyone.

After getting him settled, she got herself ready and slid under the covers. They were planning to ride into Wichita Falls in the morning. She was starting to wander if it wouldn't be too much for him. She wanted to sell her dress and buy material to learn how to sew her own dresses and other frilly things. She had planned to speak with Russell before the trip hoping he didn't care that she had lied.

Yet, what man wants a liar for a wife? She was determined to sell the fancy dress and buy material as if that one act will keep her here. What if he sent her away? It would all be for nothing.

Her head was spinning with all kinds of conclusions.

Naomi spent most of the night worrying about the outcome instead of sleeping. Beside her, Russell slept like dead weight, his steady breathing finally helping her to relax and fall asleep.

# Chapter 10

Russell pulled the buggy up to the mercantile in Wichita Falls. He watched as Naomi carefully picked up her dress and went in to speak with the proprietor. She told him it would be awhile and she'd meet him at Jenna's Café. He enjoyed seeing her so happy. She was excited to be able to trade in her exuberant gown for more simple material.

He wondered when she was going to let the cat out of the bag. He felt bad about last night. The day had gone well but he had spent too much time at the neighboring ranch, doing more than he realized. The other men had warned him not to overdo it but after he had eaten such a fine meal, the moment he sat on the rocker, he was finished.

Russell had asked her if she wanted to talk this morning but she busied herself making breakfast and cleaning up they didn't get a chance to. On the way in she was so excited about everything, she kept chatting away. First it was about the dress, the kind of material she wanted and then the waterfall when they passed it. He didn't have the heart to bring up the subject again and had a suspicion she'd rather forget she ever had a past.

If she never told him, he didn't care. Yet, somehow, he knew she cared. She kept trying to tell him but something or someone always interrupted them. Perhaps he'd be the one to bring it up on this trip at some point. He'd be honest and tell her that Miss Addie let him know. He just didn't want her to be upset with the older woman, she was a kind hearted soul that took care of everyone. Maybe she did meddle a little but sometimes, well, perhaps Miss Addie knew people better than they knew themselves.

His mind made up, Russell decided to discuss it during their lunch at the café. He began to head there when Naomi came rushing out of the mercantile, several packages in her arms. He hurried to her, taking them from her and placing them in the buggy. "That was fast."

"I thought it would take me forever to decide but when I saw the material I knew immediately what I wanted. I will be the perfect farmer's wife."

"You are the perfect farmer's wife," he told her, knowing how important it was for her to learn to sew her own clothing. It didn't matter to him, but it did to her.

"I have more news!"

"More?" He held his arm out as they made their way towards the café.

She nodded. "I'll have you know my dress sold within five minutes of being in the store. Two ladies were bidding on it and look at what else I have." She produced ten dollars. "Can you believe this?"

He shook his head. "That's a good deal. You did good for yourself."

"Thank you. Now, if I may ask a favor, I'd like to place my money in a an account at the bank. Mr. Wheeler at the mercantile told me if I put the money in an account, it will draw interest. After a while, this ten dollars becomes more. My money will grow! I can't believe it. We can save it in case we need it for the farm!"

Russell wanted to hug her. She was so excited to have a few dollars of her own. This was probably the first time she ever held that much money in her life.

She didn't need to know the farm wasn't struggling. They led a good life, had plenty and shared with others as well. He wanted her to enjoy saving her cash which made her feel needed. "I think you should put it in an account. Do you want me to go with you?"

She placed a kiss on his cheek, running her hand along the side of his face. It was the first time she acted so boldly in public or anywhere. "I would like to do this on my own if you don't mind?"

"Go on. I'll get a table and wait for you in the café."

"When I return we really do need to talk."

He nodded. "I agree."

Naomi hurried across the street, walking so fast she almost ran into the sheriff. He was crossing the street the same time she was from the opposite side.

"Morning," he told her.

"Good morning, Sheriff. It is a wonderful day!" Then she hurried up the steps to the bank and disappeared inside.

Sheriff Montana saw Russell watching his wife with a smile on his face. "She's yours?"

"She is. First time she ever held that much money in her hand. You going inside?"

"Sure am. My lovely wife gets a pastry every morning. I surprise her but by now it's not really a surprise. She knows every morning I deliver it to her door."

Russell was impressed. The sheriff ran a clean town. He didn't put up with any nonsense. He was a hardened man who didn't show much emotion. Except, evidently to his wife.

Russell got a table by the front window. He watched for some time, anxious for Naomi to get done. He knew the banker was always busy and she probably had to wait in a line but it had been well over twenty minutes.

The sheriff was leaning up against the opening that led to the kitchen talking with the cook, a tall man with a friendly face.

Everything happened so fast. A man came in the door of the café calling for the sheriff. Montana pushed himself away from the wall.

"What is it Shorty?"

The small man leaned forward, his chest heaving. "I was in the bank cleaning the office in the back. Two men are about to rob it. I got out the window above the desk and ran to your office but your deputy said you were here."

"Go on and tell my deputy what's going on and to check the immediate area. Don't look suspicious. I'm sure there are look out men outside watching everyone."

"My wife is inside." Fear ripped through Russell like he had never dealt with before. He wasn't about to sit by and wait for the sheriff to handle things. He shot out of his seat and went for the door, not looking back when the sheriff ordered him to stop.

Russell stomped across the street, noticing a cluster of horses next to the hotel. One man stood between two of the horses, possibly a look out. Russell kept walking. He pulled some bills out of his pocket, holding them flat in his hand. It appeared that he was going to deposit them. He pushed his hat back, noticing a man hanging around by the front door of the bank. "Morning," he offered.

The man stared at him hard. Russell stared back. Then the stranger nodded. "Morning," he mumbled and turned away.

Russell pushed his way through the doors. There were four townsfolk waiting in line in front of the teller. "There you are, darling!"

Naomi turned to him with a puzzled look on her face. She waved and smiled but seemed concerned. "I'll be done soon. I'm sorry it is taking so long."

"No worries, little darling. I'll wait over there." Russell pointed to a seating area against the far wall. A man sat in one of the high-back chairs, his wide brimmed hat low over his eyes. It was hard to see his face. Russell was certain the man was up to no good. They hadn't struck yet. He was hoping to get Naomi out of the bank before they did.

He took a seat in the empty chair, trying to observe his surroundings. How many men were inside? He knew for sure the one next to him was definitely an outlaw. Then he noticed the man standing behind Naomi. Russell had his eyes on her the whole time so he never noticed the outlaw behind her. She was too close for his comfort. He had to do something. Soon.

Sweat poured from his brow. He needed to get her out of there now. Russell moved his foot to stand up when the door opened again and this time the sheriff walked in. He wore no badge or tell-tale signs of who he was. Even his shirt was different. He wore a working man's shirt but it was evident Montana was no one to trifle with. Russell was sure he'd be armed.

It gave him hope if he wasn't able to get Naomi out of the bank. He stood slowly. "I better get my wife moving. I can't sit here all day. She's going to have to come back later. You married?" He turned to the outlaw.

"Nope."

"Too bad. It's great except for times like this."

The outlaw was staring a hole through his back as Russell made his way to his wife. Before he got a chance to pull her out of the way, the outlaw in the chair stood.

He pulled his guns. "Everyone, let's all drop to the floor, this here is a hold-up!"

Two patrons had just walked in, saw the gun and fled back through the way they came in.

The outlaw with the wide-brimmed hat swore. "Where the hell is Nace? He's supposed to be our lookout!" When he got to the front door and didn't see anyone keeping an eye on them, he turned quick as a whip realizing they had been found out.

He aimed his gun right as a shot rang out. The outlaw fell back against the glass window and slumped to the floor. Two ladies screamed.

That left one other outlaw inside.

The man was quick. Russell thought he had Naomi out of the way but the outlaw grabbed her and pulled her up against him pointing a gun at her throat.

Naomi's eyes went wide. Instead of fear, her eyes filled with anger. those blue orbs flashing like a wild cat caught in a corner. Russell took a step closer. His fists were balled at his sides.

"Stop, mister. Ain't no harm come to her if you stay back. Now both of you let me go out that door and I'll let the lady free."

"That ain't gonna happen, you yellow-bellied sliver of a coward. I ain't going nowhere with you and if you don't let me go, I'm going to give you something you will never forget!"

He snarled, pushing the gun closer. "You shut it up! You ain't in no position to give me orders!"

Russell silently pleaded with her, staring hard. He didn't want her to get hurt. His feet were planted on the floor ready to spring at the two of them. Russell prayed to keep her safe.

Naomi wasn't about to take this lying down. At that moment he feared for her very life.

"I am sick and tired of a measly nobody like you trying to steal from honest citizens. I lived all my life as an orphan and I hated those kids who deliberately hurt people. I saw others stabbed for a lousy dime. You didn't even get any money, what kind of bank robber are you!"

Naomi timed her last word perfectly. She lifted her foot and stomped down on the man's foot, digging her heel into his toes. He lowered the gun, not dropping it but it gave her time to react.

Russell sprang at the outlaw, taking Naomi by the arm and pushing her out of the way. Somehow the outlaw moved quick and tried to get out the door. Another shot rang out.

Sheriff Montana had killed both men without blinking an eye. "Ain't nobody going to rob this bank. Not today."

<> <>

"That was some fancy talking in there," Russell told her with a relieved smile. He leaned across the table, lowering his voice. The café was filled with townsfolk who wanted to talk about the attempted robbery. It seemed everyone gathered here. "Is there anything you want to talk to me about?"

When Naomi tried to pick up her cup, her hand shook so bad it rattled against the saucer. Russell reached across the table, placing a hand over hers. She sighed, letting out a low moan. "I guess I do," she told him, afraid to look at him, worried what she would see.

"Under any other circumstance, I would probably tease you silly until you told me the truth about your past. Not today. I already know, Naomi."

She looked at him then. His eyes weren't angry. They weren't ashamed of her when he gazed back at her. No. He was watching her with such an intense look. "You do?"

He nodded once. "Yes."

"How did you figure it out?"

"Hey." He lifted her chin with his hand. "Look at me, Naomi. I don't care about your past. I love you for who you are now, not then."

"I lied to you. Gave you false pretences. You were expecting a well to do bride. How can an orphan make you a better man? I can't barely cook and now I can't even save money without getting held up at the bank!" Tears began to stream down her face.

"We need to have this conversation somewhere else." Russell threw money on the table for the coffee and headed out of town. Russell didn't speak, he held her hand and when they got to the water falls, he stopped there and turned to her. "Naomi. I want you to stop degrading yourself. I love you. You are my wife. Maybe you can't cook and the first meal was a disaster but you are learning."

"The first meal was more than a disaster." She laughed through her tears. "I know how to use the hot iron and next week Miss Addie will teach me to sew. We were to meet up every Tuesday but then your Ma got hurt and then you almost got struck by lightening. I saw her in the mercantile and she agreed they were good enough excuses not to show."

She was talking a mile a minute. He swooped in and pressed his mouth over hers. She didn't know if it was to quiet her or because he wasn't able to resist.

Russell held her in his arms for some time. The water cascading against the rocks was almost like a serenade. They sat in the buggy with their arms around each other, watching the water, enjoying the late afternoon.

"Russell?"

"Yes."

"I love you."

"I was wondering when you were going to tell me. Thought maybe you'd keep those three words a secret."

She smiled at him, kissing him back. "Never again. I'm not holding back. Maybe you will learn something from this orphan. It's funny now, all of a sudden, I'm not ashamed. I feel as if a heavy weight has been lifted."

"I'm glad. We probably should tell Ma. That's if you want to." Russell pulled her closer.

"Your mother figured me out already. I promised I'd tell you. She didn't think it would make a difference. Turns out she was right."

Russell laughed. "Maybe it's because of all the secrets from our past. If you want to know about secrets, Naomi, wait until you hear the story about our families. It's quite an exciting tale."

"I can't wait. I want to sit outside on the porch with you, drink lemonade and star-gaze every single night for the rest of our lives."

Russell sent the buggy rolling. "Let's go home."

She snuggled against him as they went down the road. She finally had a place of her own. This little orphan girl finally did all right for herself.

"Yes, dear husband. Let's go home."

<><>

Thank you for reading Russell's story. Stay tuned for twin brother Wesley's story next.

Here's a small dose of A Bride for Wesley:[1] (https://amzn.to/ 2N3NDAr)

"It's my turn."

"Indeed. Please, come in and have a seat at my table. Tea?" Miss Addie held the door wide open.

Wesley knew it was a matter of time before his mother and Nora White sent him to Miss Addie to match him up with a bride. He'd been looking forward to it, actually. After seeing how his twin brother found a good woman, Wesley was anxious to get started.

Six months after Russell married, his mother and step-mother sat him down at their kitchen table for a *talk.*

Wesley loved life. He was content with his farm and wanted to share it with someone. Most of all, he wanted a companion for his mother. It had to be lonely for her living on a farm with two sons for so many years.

"I understand your brother is well pleased with his bride."

Wesley nodded. "Yes, ma'am. My mothers told me it was time to do the same thing. I can't wait, to tell the truth."

A smile played across Miss Addie's lips before she took a sip of her tea. Wesley noticed how dainty the china cup was, afraid to pick it up until he saw his hostess grab it with both her hands and grin. "How may I help you, Mr. Young?"

He picked up the fragile cup in one hand and took a slurp. Just one slurp. He much preferred the strong aroma of coffee brewed on the cook stove. "I appreciate you taking time to see me at such short notice. I felt led to visit after Ma and Nora sat me down for a good talking to last week. Again.

---

1. https://amzn.to/2N3NDAr

Figured I gave 'em enough time to worry they wouldn't be getting another bride in the family."

Miss Addie cocked her head. "You are quite the troublemaker, I see that in your eyes."

He nodded and smiled. "Sure am. Those two have been meddling me for the last six months. Actually, from the day my brother got married they've been wanting to match me up with someone. I always had every intention of doing so but it was too much fun making them wonder. A man has to have some fun now and again. The farm life can get monotonous if you don't try to shake things up a bit. Ma finally called me to the table and said she was tired of me playing around."

"The good news is I have the perfect bride for you. Would you care to read the letter she sent?"

"How do you know she's the right one?"

"Gut instincts, Mr. Young. This one needs a man like you to bring some sunshine and laughter into her life."

A frown appeared on Wesley's face. He didn't want some old sourpuss who never laughed. That wouldn't do. It would suck the life right out of him. "I guess I can take a look."

"Why don't I show you her photo first."

Miss Addie stood and went to the side board where a small box sat on top of a doily. She rummaged around first before pulling a letter from the pile. "I believe this is the one."

Wesley took the envelope, noticing a small photo inside. When he turned it over, his eyes popped open. "She's stunning!"

"Yes, she is quite the lady. If you will excuse me, I'll return shortly."

He hadn't even noticed when the matchmaker left the room. Wesley was still staring at the woman in the photograph. Her blonde hair, stretched back into a neat bun showed a flawless face that stared right through him. He didn't want to turn away.

Wesley wanted to stare at her all day. Did he even care what was in the letter? Her high cheekbones accented her large eyes, so blue it looked like you'd want to fall in to her soul. Her dress was immaculate, white with traces of lace on the sleeves and a blend of colors in the skirt. She stood tall and proud. A necklace made of felt was wrapped around her slender neck, with a silver cross hanging down the middle. A small pearl sat in the center of the cross. It looked expensive and from the Victorian era.

He swallowed. Wesley knew he had to read the letter. No matter how much she bewitched him, this lovely woman had to be perfect not only for him but for his ma. It probably sounded crazy, but he wanted his mother to be happy, too. If she had a companion, Wesley had done his job as a good son.

Knowing his ma would want him to be sure this was the right bride, he tore open the letter.

*Dear Miss Addie,*

*You have been highly recommended as a woman with impeccable and uncanny ways to find me the perfect match. My name is Olivia Morris, daughter of a well-known, prominent businessman here in Dallas. He wishes to marry me off to an unpleasant fellow who is guilty of crimes that I may not speak of in a correspondence letter. Perhaps the hardest reality is my father is insisting upon this marriage.*

*I am at the age where I've decided to take the bull by the horns and find a husband who has the same hopes and dreams as I. Here is my extended list of must haves, I hope that you will be able to find a suitable match.*

*1. Handsome. Or, at least pleasant to look at. And kind if the two can be found in one person.*

*2. I need someone who owns a farm or ranch.*

*3. A man who loves children.*

*4. A husband who doesn't frown upon a wife wanting to make her own way.*

*5. A place large enough for room for orphans.*

*If these can be applied, please send for me and I will come immediately to be married. Another reason I chose your agency besides your one hundred percent success rate is because of the thirty day clause in the contract.*

*Sincere wishes, Miss Olivia Morris*

Wesley looked at his reflection in the mirror above the side board. He wasn't hard to look at. He owned a farm, along with his ma and brother, so another plus in his favor. She wanted a man who loves children. Well, that was easy. He loved all children.

"Have you decided?" Miss Addie entered from the other room.

"Seems I have a fair chance. Except I'm not sure what the last two conditions are all about."

"I believe Miss Morris is independent, much like most of the brides here in Wichita Falls. The last part about the orphans, we can ask her if you decide to chose her as a bride."

"She is lovely to look at, that's for sure."

"Now, Mr. Young, looks are not everything, although it is nice to have a pleasant face to look at. Is it your wish to continue?"

"I do believe so. I'm sure my ma will be happy. And, Miss Nora."

Miss Addie leaned over, staring at him. "What about you, Mr. Young. Do you have any doubts at all for yourself?"

Wesley didn't think so. It was good there was a clause in the contract he was about to sign. He didn't want to have some bossy, rich girl making his life miserable. At least they'd have thirty days to annul the marriage if it didn't work out.

He nodded. "I'll take her."

"Indeed. I'll send you details for her arrival."

Wesley wasn't sure how he felt leaving the matchmaker's home. He was elated to be getting married. After all, a wife to come home to every night would be pleasant. He hoped she didn't want him to spend too much time with her, he loved working his farm. That's what his ma was for. The two ladies will have each other.

He was looking forward to the fun times they'd have.

Fun, happy times. No worries. Nothing to keep them from enjoying life. That seemed to be his train of thought. Never worry, just enjoy life.

He left Wichita Falls in a hurry to tell his brother Russell what he had done. He also wanted to see the looks on both mothers' faces when they finally realized he listened to them and ordered a mail order bride.

## A Bride for [2]Wesely[3] is Available Now![4]

(https://www.amazon.com/gp/product/B07GMYXL3G)

<> <> <> <> <>

Would you like to be notified when a new book comes out plus get a free book? Please sign up at Cyndiraye.com[5]

---

2. https://www.amazon.com/gp/product/B07GMYXL3G

3. https://www.amazon.com/gp/product/B07GMYXL3G

4. https://www.amazon.com/gp/product/B07GMYXL3G

5. http://www.cyndiraye.com

# Don't miss out!

Visit the website below and you can sign up to receive emails whenever Cyndi Raye publishes a new book. There's no charge and no obligation.

https://books2read.com/r/B-A-PXQ-ADWFC

**BOOKS 2 READ**

Connecting independent readers to independent writers.